Listen
—for the—
Whippoorwill

Dave & Neta Jackson

Story illustrations by
Julian Jackson

BETHANY HOUSE PUBLISHERS
MINNEAPOLIS, MINNESOTA 55438

Published by Bethany House Publishers
11400 Hampshire Avenue South
Bloomington, Minnesota 55438

Bethany House Publishers is a division of
Baker Publishing Group, Grand Rapids, Michigan.

Printed in the United States of America

Library of Congress Cataloging-in-Publication Data

Jackson, Dave.
    Listen for the whippoorwill / Dave & Neta Jackson.
       p. cm. — (Trailblazer books)
    Summary: A young slave girl on a Maryland plantation is led to
freedom by Harriet Tubman.
      1. Tubman, Harriet 1820?–1913—Juvenile fiction. [1.–Tubman,
Harriet 1820?–1913—Fiction. 2. Slavery—Fiction. 3. Afro-
Americans—Fiction. 4. Christian life—Fiction.] I. Jackson, Neta.
II. Jackson, Julian, Ill. III. Title. IV. Series.
PZ7.J132418Li   1993
[Fic]—dc20   93–26837
ISBN 1–55661–272–9   CIP
                                    AC

All the historical facts and information about Harriet Tubman in this story are true. Rosebud and her family, the little band of runaways, and the Quaker family depicted in this story, while not actual people, are based on typical people and events that happened while Harriet Tubman was a "conductor" on the Underground Railroad. Thomas Garrett, the Quaker abolitionist, and William Still, secretary for the Vigilance Committee in Philadelphia, were also real people who aided Harriet Tubman and the slaves' journey to freedom on the Underground Railroad.

CONTENTS

DAVE AND NETA JACKSON are a full-time husband/wife writing team who have authored and coauthored many books on marriage and family, the church, relationships, and other subjects. Their books for children include the TRAILBLAZER series and *Hero Tales* Volumes I, II, III, and IV. The Jacksons have two married children, Julian and Rachel, and make their home in Evanston, Illinois.

Chapter 1

The Stranger

LEANING OVER THE EDGE of the rain barrel, Rosebud plunged the wooden bucket into the water. Hauling with all her strength, the girl then heaved the heavy bucket over the edge, spilling half of the water in the process—most of it on herself.

Rosebud cussed under her breath, then looked quickly around to see if Mammy had heard. But she could still hear her mother singing inside the cookhouse:

Climbin' up the mountain, children.
Didn't come here for to stay,
If ah nevermore see you again,
Gonna meet you at de judgment day.

Sarah Jackson was cook for the Big House on the old Powers Plantation, and twelve-year-old Rosebud had been helping her mother as long as she could remember. Today was bread-baking day and Rosebud's job was to scrub out the big pots that the dough had been mixed in.

Sloshing water over her bare feet with every step, the girl carried the bucket over to the pots lying on the grass. April clouds hid the sun and she shivered in the cool Maryland air. Rosebud hated baking day, and she especially hated scrubbing out the dough pots. Gooey flour clung in great clumps to the sides, and scrub as she might, it never seemed to come off.

Rosebud was working on her second pot when she heard hoofbeats. Even though the cookhouse stood behind the Big House, from where Rosebud was working she could just see the long, tree-lined lane leading up to the Big House. A lone horseman was riding up the lane. She didn't recognize the man or the horse.

"Isaac!" she yelled. "Isaac! You better make tracks. Horseman comin'!"

Fifteen-year-old Isaac appeared from behind the cookhouse. "I seed him," he hissed at her as he trotted past. "Don't be telling me my business." Then he disappeared around the front of the house to hold the stranger's horse while the man dismounted.

Isaac was stable boy for the Powers Plantation. Rosebud knew her older brother liked taking care of the riding horses, but he had a bad habit of sneaking off to catch crawdads in the creek below the stable.

Once Mr. Powers couldn't find Isaac when he wanted his horse; Isaac had been given a terrible whipping when he was found asleep in the straw. "Fool boy gonna get us all on the auction block," Rosebud's pappy had muttered. Abe Jackson was Mr. Power's top field hand, but he didn't mess with "Massa Powers." Frightened, Rosebud had taken it upon herself after that to be Isaac's eyes and ears and let him know when he was wanted.

A few minutes later she saw Isaac run back toward the stable. Curious, Rosebud dropped her scrub brush and walked cautiously along the side of the Big House, being careful to keep out of sight. The stranger talking to Mr. Powers was square-jawed and stocky, with a full head of white hair. From behind the bushes she could just make out what he was saying.

"President Fillmore is finally enforcing the Fugitive Slave Law—which makes my job easier." The man spit out a stream of tobacco juice, threw back his head, and laughed. "But it makes them Nigra-lovers up north crazy mad."

"I don't need a slave catcher." Mr. Powers sounded annoyed. "My slaves are very loyal."

Rosebud saw the stranger take a long, critical survey of the buildings on the plantation. The cookhouse, stable, tobacco barns, weaving shed, and the rows of tiny cabins hidden among the trees in the slave quarters all looked tired and weather-beaten. Even the Big House needed a coat of paint.

"Waal," the man drawled, spitting again, "I'm

buyin' slaves, too—need 'em for a chain gang down South, clearin' forest land for crops. I can pay a good price."

"I'm not eager to sell any of my slaves if I can help it," said Mr. Powers curtly. "But if cotton and tobacco prices keep falling . . . I may be forced to do something." He shrugged. Just then Isaac reappeared with Mr. Powers' big bay horse, all saddled and bridled. "Ah! Here's my horse. We can take a look at some of the slaves if you like, but I'm not making any promises."

But as Mr. Powers put his boot in the left stirrup and started to swing into his saddle, the saddle slipped.

Before Rosebud knew what was happening, Mr. Powers had whirled angrily on Isaac. "You good-for-nothing boy!" he yelled, striking her brother about the head again and again with his riding crop. "Are you trying to break my neck? Maybe you'd rather work a chain gang down South, eh?"

With an angry jerk, Mr. Powers tightened the saddle girth and rode off with the stranger toward the tobacco fields. Rosebud could see Isaac fighting back angry tears. Looking around, the boy saw his sister watching from the corner of the Big House. Upset that someone had witnessed his humiliation, Isaac ran around the Big House and took off through the trees toward the creek.

Rosebud was scared and raced back to the cookhouse. "Mammy!" she cried, trembling. Sarah Jackson was just sliding a long wooden paddle out of the oven with four loaves of golden bread, steaming and fragrant. The older woman straightened. Her black face, framed with a blue bandana tied around her head, shone with sweat. It was obvious that she was heavy with child, soon to give birth.

Words tumbled out in a rush as Rosebud told what had just happened. "Is Massa Powers gonna sell Isaac to a chain gang?" the girl cried, fear in her eyes.

Sarah wiped her face with the bottom of her apron. "Hush, now, girl. Massa Powers was just embarrassed to be made a fool of in front of a stranger," she said. "He prob'ly didn't mean nothin' by it." But she went to the door of the cookhouse and looked anxiously in the direction of the creek.

Rosebud pleaded to go look for Isaac, but Sarah ordered her to finish cleaning the dough pots. Rosebud could hardly keep her mind on her work. What if Isaac had run away? What if he wasn't there to unsaddle Mr. Powers' horse when he came back?

She'd heard tales whispered fearfully among the slaves about the dogs sent after a runaway. She had to find Isaac!

But when the pots were finally drying on the grass, it was time for Rosebud, along with Phoebe— a young slave woman whom Sarah was training to be a cook—to help prepare supper for the folks in the Big House.

By the time the last steaming pot of oyster stew and fresh bread had been delivered to the serving maids at the back door of the Big House, daylight was almost gone. With heart thumping, Rosebud ran to the stable. Mr. Powers' horse was in its stall munching the hay in the manger . . . and there was Isaac, cleaning Mr. Powers' saddle with oil. But even in the half-light, Rosebud could see an angry welt from the riding whip alongside Isaac's eye.

Isaac refused to look at her. With exaggerated slowness, he put away the oil and cleaning rag and hung up the saddle. He closed the stable door, slid the latch, then sauntered carelessly toward the creek. Without a word, Rosebud followed two steps behind.

This was a familiar ritual. Around the cookhouse and stable and yard—and especially around the white folks—Isaac wore an invisible mask, and even ignored his younger sister. But almost every evening, Isaac and Rosebud waded in the creek or walked noiselessly—like Indians—in the woods. Then Isaac would talk, pointing out which berries were poisonous, showing her how to catch crawdads without getting pinched, how to tell direction by the moss

growing on the north side of the big oak trees.

Walking behind Isaac, Rosebud let out a sigh. Her brother hadn't run away. They were walking to the creek as usual. Maybe everything was going to be all right.

But Isaac was quieter tonight. He just sat on the bank of the creek and watched it flowing west, gurgling its way toward Chesapeake Bay, which neither of them had ever seen even though it was only ten miles away. Like many slaves on the Eastern Shore of Maryland, the Jackson family had rarely been off the plantation, and then only to go into town on an errand.

As twilight deepened, Rosebud heard a friendly bird call. It sounded like, *Whip-poor-will. Whip-poor-will*. "The whippoorwill's back!" She grinned. The little brown-speckled bird hid quietly among the dead leaves on the ground during the day, and only woke up as night approached. This was the first one she'd heard this spring.

The stars started coming out. Pointing a finger at the sky, Isaac finally spoke. "See the Big Dipper there?"

Rosebud looked through the bare branches of the trees, which hadn't started to leaf yet, and nodded.

"If you follow the two stars that make the drinkin' edge of the Dipper, they point straight at the North Star . . . see?"

Rosebud nodded again as she picked out the bright star.

" 'Follow the North Star' . . . that's what they

say," Isaac murmured. "'Follow the North Star to freedom.'"

Rosebud didn't like the tone of Isaac's voice—wishful and stubborn at the same time. She hoped he wasn't thinking what she thought he was thinking.

When the two children finally crept into the log cabin in the slave quarters, Sarah and Abe Jackson were sitting by the smoky fireplace talking in low voices. ". . . saw Massa and that slave trader from Charleston looking over the field hands," Abe was saying.

"I know Massa's worried about money, but you don't think he'd start selling off slaves, do you? How's he gonna get the crops in?"

"I dunno. In these bad times, some slave owners raise slaves to sell just like another cash crop. And Massa Powers—he sho' is wound up tight these days. Ain't like it used to be."

"Hush," warned Sarah, glancing at the children. Rising awkwardly, one hand on her swollen belly, Sarah fished out two tin plates, which she had kept warm in the ashes, and handed them to Isaac and Rosebud. Hungrily, the two children sucked the meat off the small smoked fish and stuffed corn bread into their mouths. As they lay down on the straw-stuffed mattresses on the floor and pulled up the thin blankets, Sarah began to sing softly:

Hush. Hush. Somebody's callin' mah name.
Sounds like Jesus. Somebody's callin'
mah name.

The last thing Rosebud remembered was her mammy's soothing voice . . .

I'm so glad. Trouble don't last always.
Oh, mah Lawd, what shall I do?

Rosebud woke with a start. The cabin was empty and sunlight was streaming through the chinks in the logs. Grabbing a piece of cold corn bread, the girl ran through the trees to the cookhouse. She saw Mr. Powers riding down the front lane on his big bay. Her mother and Phoebe already had the fire built in the oven and were mixing biscuit dough.

"Where's Isaac?" Rosebud asked.

"In the stable where he belongs, doin' chores," said her mother. "Now wash your hands and face and fry up that piece of side meat. Miz Powers be wantin' her breakfast soon . . . Phoebe! Don't stir those biscuits so hard. Gotta do it gentle-like."

Rosebud smirked. Phoebe was twenty years old and had been working with the field hands until last week. But Mr. Powers' overseer thought the attractive young black woman distracted the male slaves from their work, so he moved her to the cookhouse—much to Sarah Jackson's dismay. "Rosebud is a better cook than that hussy," she had complained to her husband.

Later that morning, while Rosebud was plucking feathers from a freshly butchered chicken, she heard childish laughter. The Powers' children, two girls about four and six, were playing tag in back of the Big House. Nanny Sue, one of the house slaves, was watching over them. Rosebud wondered what it would be like to wear ribbons in her hair and dress in a fine cotton dress with a ruffled petticoat. She had never talked to the two little girls. Only the house-maids and Old Jim, the butler, were allowed to associate with the Powers family or to enter the Big House.

Just then Rosebud saw Isaac ride by the cookhouse on a young chestnut horse he'd been break-ing in for Mrs. Powers. "Isaac!" she called, but he continued at an easy trot down the wide front lane.

"Where's Isaac goin', Mammy?"

"Now, how would I know?" Sarah said impa-tiently. "Miz Powers prob'ly sendin' him on an er-rand. You stick to your pluckin'—Massa Powers bringin' guests home tonight and we got two more chickens to do."

When Mr. Powers arrived in late afternoon ac-companied by two men on horseback and two ladies in an open carriage, three fried chickens were crisp and golden on a platter warming by the stove and a pot of black-eyed peas and rice—known as Hoppin' John—was bubbling over the fire.

"Isaac!" yelled Mr. Powers. Rosebud saw her mother go to the cookhouse door and glance anx-iously toward the stable. They hadn't seen Isaac return on the chestnut horse.

Just then they heard Old Jim's voice. "I seed the

boy go off on the Missus' horse, Massa Powers," said the aging butler, out of earshot of the guests who were dismounting and going into the house. "Thought you'd sent him off on an errand."

"No . . ." Mr. Powers' voice was irritated. "But maybe Mrs. Powers did. Will you ask her please, Jim, when she expects him to return? I need him to rub down these horses for our guests."

Old Jim returned a moment later and shook his head silently. Mr. Powers' face went dark. He held an angry conference in a low voice with Old Jim, then stomped furiously into the house. Another slave soon appeared to take care of the horses and carriage, and yet another was sent into town on horseback, riding at breakneck speed.

By the time the sun had set, there wasn't a slave on the Powers Plantation that didn't know that young Isaac Jackson had run away, riding off on his mistress's horse in broad daylight.

Chapter 2

Runaway!

ABE JACKSON, bone-tired from plowing the winter-hard soil, ran immediately to the cookhouse when he heard the news. Sarah was rocking herself on a stool in silent distress. Rosebud, curled unhappily in a corner, saw her pappy pat his wife awkwardly on the shoulder.

"That Isaac's a fool!" he spat out, shaking his head. "He's tryin' to cross the Red Sea all by hisself. He shoulda waited." Abe's voice lowered to a whisper. " 'Cause I been hearing that there's someone they call Moses, leadin' our people to the Promised Land up north on some kind o' railroad that goes underground."

"Don't talk 'bout any Moses!" moaned Sarah. "Ol' Nat Turner thought he was Moses, and it weren't long 'til he got hisself killed."

"Huh!" snorted Phoebe with a wicked grin. "Not afore he done killed a lot of white folks first!"

"What do you know about it?" Sarah snapped at the young woman. "Happened a year or two afore you were even born. Lots o' things changed after Nat Turner tried to get the slaves stirred up. Black folks ain't allowed to go to church together or teach their kids the Bible. Can't teach the younguns to read or write. Can't even sing 'bout Moses! White folks is scared."

Rosebud strained to hear the low talk of the grownups. She never realized what a risk her mother was taking when, night after night, she told Bible stories about Moses and King David and Jesus after Rosebud and Isaac had lain down on their mats. She always thought the reason Mammy whispered was to help them go to sleep.

But . . . did Pappy mean there was a new Moses? And what kind of railroad went underground?

Rosebud's thoughts were interrupted by a commotion outside. Opening the cookhouse door a crack, the Jacksons and Phoebe could see three men on horseback—Mr. Powers and the two gentlemen who came for supper—trying to control their excited horses. Old Jim was holding a flaming torch, which cast dancing shadows all about the stableyard.

Rosebud's heart pounded as another figure rode into the torchlight. A shout went up. "Here he is! We can go after the runaway now."

The white-haired slave catcher had returned.

The ground seemed to shake as the little band kicked their horses into a gallop past the cookhouse and down the front lane. Old Jim disappeared with the torch, and all of a sudden a quiet darkness fell over the yard and buildings of the Powers Plantation. Not a slave was to be seen.

Back in their tiny cabin, Rosebud lay stiffly on her mat, ears straining to catch any sound from outside. *Run, Isaac, run!* she thought. *Don't let them catch you!* Then the other part of her heart cried silently, *Come home, Isaac. Don't go away. Who will go walking with me down by the creek? Who will be my friend?*

Sometime during the night, she heard a muffled sound. Her mother was crying. "Lord, Lord," she heard Mammy moan, "what's goin' to happen to my boy?"

Rosebud drifted off to sleep, but she awoke with a jerk. Hoofbeats were coming down the lane. Shouts. Rough laughter. Her parents heard it, too, and leaped up from their straw mattress.

The sun wasn't up yet, but the April sky was yellow and pink with first light. Abe and Sarah, still in their nightclothes, went running hand in hand through the hickory and ash trees, past the other slave cabins toward the Big House, with Rosebud at their heels. As they reached the stable yard, the slave family stopped and froze.

Mr. Powers and the other two horsemen were dismounting. Bringing up the rear was the white-haired slave catcher holding a rope; at the end of the rope was Isaac, arms tightly bound. The boy's ankles were chained with iron fetters. But Isaac's face was a mask, showing no emotion.

Sarah gave a little cry, and Abe reached out a big arm to steady her. A few other slaves, mostly field hands heading out for work, had also appeared silently in the yard.

Mr. Powers noticed the bystanders. "Abe, get your woman and girl outta here!" he ordered. "You—" Mr. Powers pointed at one of the young field hands. "Take care of these horses. The rest of you get to work—*now!*"

As Abe drew Sarah away, Rosebud hung back, hiding in the shadow of a large hickory tree. What was going to happen to Isaac? She saw Mr. Powers turn to the slave catcher. "Give him a whippin' he won't forget!" the plantation owner said harshly. "Then chain him in the stable. I'll decide what to do with him later."

The slave catcher reached in his pocket for a fresh chew of tobacco. "This one's a troublemaker, Mr. Powers. You'd be better off without him. Just want to remind you that I'm leaving for Charleston tomorrow morning. And I pay top price for young bloods like this. A couple years on the chain gang will calm him down."

With that, the slave catcher jerked the rope, nearly pulling Isaac off his feet, then headed for the stable, chuckling to himself. The two guests slapped Mr. Powers on the back and the three men went inside the Big House.

Rosebud felt rooted to the hickory tree, not knowing what to do. A few minutes later she heard the stinging snap of a rawhide whip and an agonized scream inside the stable. It was Isaac! Putting her hands over her ears, Rosebud ran for the slave cabins.

Her parents hardly noticed as Rosebud threw

25

herself down on the straw mat and pulled the blanket over her head. Abe was holding his wife in his big arms. "Oh, Jesus, help my boy . . . help my boy," Sarah cried.

Oh, Jesus, Jesus, Rosebud echoed silently, *stop that bad man from whipping Isaac!* Then an awful thought crept into her head. *Mammy is always talking to Jesus and askin' for help . . . but why doesn't Jesus ever do anything?*

She felt her father shaking her. "Come on, now, Rosebud. You gotta help your mammy. It's near her time, you know, and she's upset. But there ain't nothin' we can do for Isaac right now. Go on . . . take your mammy up to the cookhouse. The Big House will be expectin' breakfast, same as always."

Abe pulled on his overalls and started out for the fields. Then he called back, "Rosebud! You stay away from that stable, you hear?"

The day dragged by slowly in the cookhouse. As soon as one meal was done, it was time to start the next one. Sarah was lost in her own thoughts and hardly seemed to notice Phoebe's irritating chatter. But when Phoebe returned from taking the noon meal to the Big House, she had news.

"I heard how they caught Isaac," she said smugly.

Sarah stopped cracking the shells of the boiled crabs for the crabcakes she was making. "Go on," she said, looking Phoebe in the eye.

"He musta rode that chestnut horse hard, 'cause it went lame up by Hurlock—"

"Hurlock!" said Sarah. "Why, that's only fifteen

26

miles north o' here."

"Well, a white man saw him walkin' the horse and demanded to see his travel pass. 'Course Isaac didn't have no pass, so the man hauled him into town. He figured somebody would turn up soon to claim him—and sho' enough, along comes the slave catcher and Mr. Powers in the middle of the night, and there's Isaac, all tied up waitin' for 'em. Huh!" Phoebe snorted. "Don't know why Isaac didn't hide in the woods and wait till dark."

Rosebud felt like hitting Phoebe, but her mother gave her a warning look that said, *Be careful. Don't start no trouble. Keep your feelings to yourself.*

Finally the crabcakes and baked corn had been sent up to the Big House for supper. The last of the baking pans had been washed and the cookhouse floor swept. But the field hands hadn't come in yet. Phoebe had an opinion about that: "Mr. Powers prob'ly told the overseer to work the field hands extra today, get 'em good and tired so no one else wanna run away."

As her mother and Phoebe headed back toward the slave cabins to get their own supper, Rosebud saw her opportunity. Pappy wasn't home yet, even though it was getting dark. Keeping to the shadows, the girl ducked behind the stable. She listened, but all she heard was the sound of horses munching hay. Taking a chance, she pulled open the back door of the stable and slipped inside.

It took a few minutes for her eyes to adjust to the darkness inside the stable. Then she saw Isaac, half

lying on the ground, his hands
and feet chained to a post.

Rosebud stifled the cry that
rose to her lips. Instead she
called softly, "Isaac. It's me,
Rosebud. I have supper for you."

Moving swiftly toward
her brother, Rosebud
reached out to help
him sit up. But
when she
touched
his back,
he cried
out and
cringed.
Rosebud
pulled
her hand
away; it was wet and sticky with Isaac's blood.

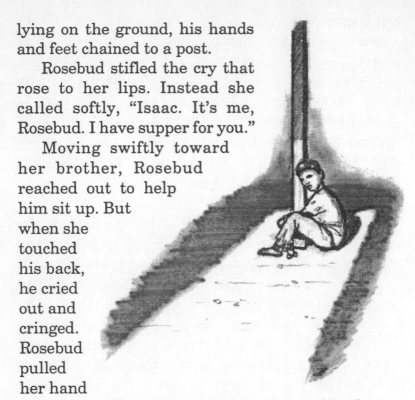

Tears sprang to her eyes, but she brushed them
away and quickly undid the knot in her apron. Carefully she held a stolen crabcake to Isaac's lips. She
half smiled in the darkness. If the Powers only knew
their supper was being fed to the runaway!

Isaac ate hungrily as she held the crabcake to his
mouth. When he'd swallowed the last bite, he whispered hoarsely, "Don't you cry 'bout me, Rosebud. I
don't care what they do. . . . I'm gonna be free."

"But why, Isaac!" Rosebud cried. "Things ain't so
bad if you don't get Mr. Powers all riled up. Why, we

got Pappy and Mammy, and she gonna have a baby soon. . . . Just be a good boy and ever'thing gonna be okay."

Isaac shook his head. "Bein' a slave ain't never okay. Now go on, git . . . don't let 'em catch you here."

Reluctantly, Rosebud stood up. As she silently let herself out the back door of the stable, Isaac's hoarse voice floated toward her in the dark: "Just remember what I said: someday I'm gonna be free!"

Chapter 3

Two Graves

ROSEBUD WAS DREAMING about catching crawdads in the creek with Isaac when her father shook her awake the next morning. Stumbling sleepily behind her mother toward the cookhouse, Rosebud wondered why she had a heavy feeling that something was wrong. Then she remembered: Isaac.

What's going to happen to him? she worried. *Will Mr. Powers keep him chained in the stable another whole day? Will he still let him be stable boy, or make him go out with the field hands? What if . . . ?* She shook the last thought out of her head. But as she lit the fire and helped her mother mix up the hasty pudding, Phoebe burst in the cookhouse door.

"That slave catcher's back—and he's got a chain gang!"

Dropping her spoon, Sarah Jackson ran out of the cookhouse door as fast as her pregnant body would move. Rosebud grabbed her skirt and dashed after her. There, coming up the lane like a king, was the slave catcher on his horse. Trailing behind him were five black slaves chained to each other by iron rings around their necks, their hands and feet also shackled with iron fetters and chains.

Rosebud whirled around and her mouth went dry. Mr. Powers was leading Isaac out of the stable and coming toward the chain gang.

The field hands, who had been walking with their hoes toward the fields, stopped and stared. Rosebud saw her pappy drop his hoe and walk unsteadily back toward the Big House. The white overseer didn't stop him.

Without a word Mr. Powers handed Isaac over to the slave catcher. Rosebud watched in shock as the man locked an iron ring around her brother's neck and chained him to the last slave in the gang. Then, with a grin, the slave catcher counted out several bills and handed them to Mr. Powers.

"You won't regret it," the stocky man beamed as he swung back up on his horse. "I'll be back. Remember what I said." He spit out a stream of brown tobacco juice and started back down the lane, the line of slaves shuffling in their chains behind him.

"No!" screamed Rosebud. "Don't take Isaac! No! No!" She would have run after him, but Phoebe grabbed her and held her fast.

Just then Rosebud's mother let out a high-pitched

cry and sank to the ground in a dead faint. Abe ran over to his wife and barked at Rosebud, "Get some water." Wrenching herself out of Phoebe's grip, Rosebud ran to the rain barrel and was back in a moment with a dipper of water, hiccupping with sobs.

As Abe held the dipper to Sarah's lips, Mr. Powers walked over. "I'm sorry about this, Abe," he said. "I didn't want to do it. But I can't have mutiny among my slaves." Mr. Powers looked around at the other slaves, who stood frozen in little groups and staring at the chain gang as it disappeared down the lane.

"Let this be a warning to you!" the plantation owner shouted. "Do your work as you're told, and we'll get this plantation back on its feet again. Now, get on about your business!"

Mr. Powers turned back to the Jackson family, knelt down, and helped Abe get Sarah back on her feet. "Take care of your woman, Abe," he said. "You lost one child; let's not lose the new one." Then the white man walked back into the Big House.

As Abe and Rosebud helped Sarah back to the cookhouse, Rosebud heard her pappy mutter something sarcastic under his breath. She wasn't sure, but it sounded like, " 'Course not, Massa. Gotta raise one more slave baby to line your pockets with money."

For days Rosebud cried whenever she thought about Isaac. His straw mattress lay empty in their little cabin in the slave quarters; now there was no one to walk with her down by the creek after the day's work was done. One of the older slaves who was worn out with field work was brought in to be the "stable boy."

Nights were the worst. In the stillness she could almost hear the rawhide whip snapping in the air and feel the wet, sticky blood on Isaac's back. Again and again he marched through her dreams, chained by his neck to the chain gang.

She wanted to tell her parents about what Isaac had said that last night, but she was afraid to admit that she had disobeyed by going to the stable. So she kept her brother's words locked in her heart: "I don't care what they do. . . . I'm gonna be free!"

Rosebud was also worried about her mother. Mammy rarely talked or smiled now while working in the cookhouse. She moved slowly and heavily, as if the burden she carried was sapping all her strength. And now and then Rosebud heard her singing mournfully in a low tone:

> *Sometimes I feel like a motherless chile*
> *Sometimes I feel like a motherless chile*
> *A long ways from home.*

About a week after Isaac had been taken away, the two women and Rosebud were working in the cookhouse when Sarah suddenly stopped in the middle of grinding dried corn into cornmeal and gave a loud groan. Gripping the edge of the wooden table, she lowered her bulky body onto a stool.

Phoebe took one look at the older woman and said, "Get the midwife, Rosebud. Hurry!"

For a moment Rosebud couldn't think. Midwife? Who was the midwife? Then she remembered: Nanny Sue, the nanny for the Powers children, was the one they always called for slave babies.

Her heart pounding, Rosebud hurried to the back door of the Big House and pulled the bell string. It seemed a long time before anyone answered, and Rosebud frantically rang the bell again. One of the housemaids finally opened the door.

"Quick, missy!" Rosebud said anxiously. "Get Nanny Sue to the cookhouse right away. My mammy gonna have her baby!"

Nanny Sue, a plump, middle-aged house slave with a golden-brown face, soon appeared and followed Rosebud to the cookhouse. She took one look at Sarah and helped the groaning woman lie down on the floor. With experienced hands, she felt Sarah's rigid stomach.

"This baby ain't right," she murmured. "It ain't turned around yet."

Frightened, Rosebud watched as the midwife massaged her mother's tummy, trying to coax the unborn child to turn around so that it could be born headfirst. The minutes dragged. From time to time Sarah gave a loud groan from the floor.

"What's the trouble here? Is this going to take long?" said a new voice. With a start, Rosebud looked up and saw Mrs. Powers standing at the doorway of the cookhouse.

"It's Sarah Jackson, Miz Powers," said Nanny Sue, still bending over the laboring woman. "It's her time, but the baby ain't right. Can't get it turned around."

"Oh dear . . ." Mrs. Powers looked flustered. "And I'm expecting the banker's wife for lunch. Do you think . . . could we move her back to her cabin? Really, the cookhouse is no place to have a baby."

Without waiting for an answer, Mrs. Powers motioned at Rosebud. "You, girl, go to the stable and ask the man to bring the wagon. He can take your mammy back to her cabin."

Reluctantly, Rosebud did as she was told. In a

short while, the wagon pulled up by the cookhouse door. Nanny Sue was shaking her head and muttering, "Shouldn't move this woman." Nonetheless, she and Phoebe helped Sarah get up and somehow got her into the back of the wagon.

Rosebud was about to hop on, too, when Mrs. Powers caught her arm. "No, girl. You need to stay here. Nanny Sue can take care of your mammy. You and Phoebe need to finish making the noon meal. Now hurry up. I'm expecting company."

Rosebud felt like jerking away and running after the wagon, but Phoebe gave her a warning look. *Do as you're told. Don't start no trouble.*

Everything seemed to take longer without Mammy. The clam chowder smelled a little scorched and the corn bread looked a little lumpy, but Rosebud hoped that Mrs. Powers wouldn't notice. Phoebe and Rosebud worked all day in the hot cookhouse. As they scrubbed the cooking pots, then started supper, Rosebud wondered anxiously if Mammy had had the baby yet and if it was all right.

Finally, at twilight, the supper dishes of fried catfish, boiled potatoes, and steamed carrots had been delivered to the back door of the Big House. Without a word, Rosebud took off running for the slave cabins, leaving Phoebe to clean up the supper pots. She had to find out what was happening!

A small crowd of slave women were gathered around the outside of the Jackson's cabin. They parted silently and let Rosebud step into the dark doorway. Her heart thumped fearfully. Was something wrong? As her eyes adjusted to the dim light, she saw Nanny Sue sitting beside her mother on the straw mattress, wiping her face with a wet cloth. Then someone else caught her eye; it was her pappy, sitting on a stool by the fireplace with a wrapped bundle in his lap.

Rosebud looked anxiously at Nanny Sue. *The baby . . . ?*

Nanny Sue shook her head. "Baby was born dead, child. A big healthy boy, but the cord was around his neck. He never made it to the light of day." She handed Rosebud the wet cloth. "Now we gotta help your mammy. She ain't doin' too good. It was a hard birth."

The next morning at daybreak, a procession of slaves wound its way through the slave cabins to a little clearing in the woods down by the creek. Abe Jackson walked at the head of the line, holding his dead baby boy wrapped in a thin cotton blanket. Rosebud followed at her father's elbow, shivering in the cool spring morning. Only Sarah was missing; she was still too weak to get up.

A small hole had been dug in the graveyard among the simple wooden crosses. As Abe laid the little body in the bottom of the grave, Old Jim began reciting the Twenty-third Psalm in a quavering voice: "The Lord is my shepherd. I shall not want . . ."

One by one the other voices joined in. "He maketh

me to lie down in green pastures: he leadeth me beside the still waters. He restoreth my soul . . ." Tears ran down Rosebud's face as the familiar words her mother had taught her filled the little clearing. ". . . Surely goodness and mercy shall follow me all the days of my life: and I will dwell in the house of the Lord for ever. Amen."

Then Abe spoke for the first time. "The baby's name is Matthew. It means 'Gift of God.' God gave me a son to replace the son I lost . . . and then God took him back again. Isaac wanted to be free. But Matthew is already free. He will never be a slave."

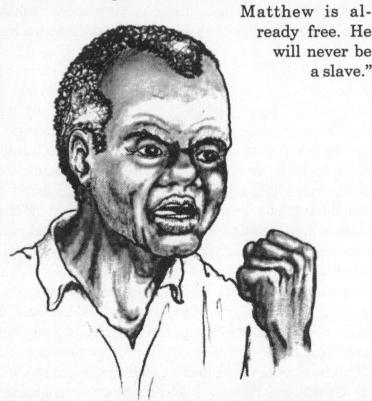

"Praise God Almighty!" a voice shouted from the crowd. Another voice burst into a song:

Thank God a'mighty, I'm free at last.
Surely been 'buked, and surely been scorned,
Thank God a'mighty, I'm free at last.
But still my soul is-a heaven born,
Thank God a'mighty, I'm free at last.

As they sang, several field hands shoveled dirt into the little grave and patted it into a smooth mound. Then the group of slaves quietly broke up and disappeared through the trees, back to the day's work.

Rosebud went to work in the cookhouse with Phoebe, aching inside. If only Mammy would get better! Mammy would make everything all right again.

But Sarah did not get better. Abe and Rosebud had to hold up her head to feed her warm broth several times a day. Sometimes she tossed feverishly on the bed and called out, "Where's my baby?" Then Abe would gently remind her that the baby was home in heaven with Jesus.

Even Mr. Powers stopped by the little cabin to see how Sarah was doing. He stood awkwardly on the dirt floor, turning his hat in his hands. That same day he rode down the lane on his big bay horse and returned with the doctor from town.

The doctor shook his head. "This woman's got a fever—an infection from childbirth. She might make

39

it, she might not. We'll have to just wait and see."

The first day of May was "issue day," when all the
slaves lined up after work to get their monthly ra-
tion of basic foodstuffs: flour, cornmeal, dried pork
rinds, salted fish, salt. Rosebud was so worried about
her mammy she barely noticed that the rations were
skimpier than usual. Of course without Isaac their
family was smaller; but the overseer barked at the
complaining slaves, "Got bad times ahead; every-
body gotta tighten their belts."

Work in the cookhouse was hard without her
mother. Mrs. Powers frequently sent complaints
about food that wasn't properly cooked or didn't taste
right. "Oh, please, Mammy, get well," Rosebud whispered as she stumbled home at night, dead tired. "I
need you."

But less than two weeks after they buried baby
Matthew, another sad procession wound its way
through the woods to the little clearing. A larger hole
had been dug beside the tiny grave; this time, four
men lowered Sarah's body into the ground. This
time, Abe did not say anything; he just stared mutely
as the men shoveled dirt into the grave.

Grief seemed to stick in Rosebud's throat; her
eyes were bright with hot, unshed tears. Isaac was
gone . . . the new baby was dead . . . and now her
mother, too. It was too much. Her feelings seemed
frozen inside of her. She heard the mournful voices

singing, "Deep river, my home is over Jordan . . ." as if they were far away.

As Abe and Rosebud turned away from the grave, they saw Mr. Powers watching from the edge of the clearing. He cleared his throat as they approached.

"I'm mighty sorry, Abe," he said, twisting his hat in his hands. "Your Sarah was a good woman. We will miss her." Then Mr. Powers put on his hat and walked off.

"Miss her cookin', you mean," Rosebud hissed when he was out of hearing.

To her surprise, her pappy didn't scold her. Abe had a strange, hard look on his face.

"You gonna pay for this, Massa Powers, *sir*," he said in a low voice. "Because you done broke my Sarah's heart when you sold Isaac to the chain gang."

Chapter 4

Moses Is Back!

ROSEBUD AND PHOEBE TRIED to keep up with the cooking for the Big House, but it was too much. The cookhouse had to turn out three meals a day for Mr. and Mrs. Powers and their two children, Old Jim the butler, Nanny Sue, four housemaids, and any guests.

One of the housemaids told Phoebe, who told Rosebud, that Mrs. Powers had thrown a fit when she heard that Sarah had died. "We train a good cook and take care of her and let her raise a family, and then she abandons us!" the white woman had stormed to her husband. "The least she could have done was produce a live brat. Now we've lost three slaves in three weeks—all named *Jackson!*"

"Now, Martha—" Mr. Powers had tried to interrupt. But Mrs. Powers was on the warpath.

"And what do we have left? A skinny child and a field hand cooking for the Powers! We'll be the laughingstock of the Eastern Shore."

"Who's doing the cooking is the least of our worries," Mr. Powers had snapped (according to the maid). "The bank is leaning on me to repay the loan we took out for the south quarter. If tobacco prices don't turn around this year, I may have to sell off some land . . . or some of the slaves."

Rosebud didn't tell her pappy what Mrs. Powers had said about her mammy, but she did tell him what Mr. Powers said about the bank.

Danger of frost was past and it was seedtime. Abe Jackson and the other field hands worked from sunup to sundown putting in tobacco, cotton, and corn. It was also time for the slaves to plant the little vegetable gardens around the cabins and in the sunny patches between the trees for their own food: collard greens and sweet potatoes, squash and carrots, peas and string beans. There was no time during seedtime for walking by the creek after work, but that was just as well for Rosebud. Walking in the woods reminded her too much of Isaac.

Then, a week after her mother had been buried, Mr. Powers hired a white woman from town to come help with the cooking. Mrs. Bumper, the new cook, had her own way of cooking. When Phoebe or Rosebud tried to do things the way Rosebud's mammy had taught them, Mrs. Bumper yelled at them. She seemed offended to be working with slave girls and made it very clear that she was the boss. "I may be hired out," she sniffed the first day, "but don't you nigger girls forget who your betters are."

The second day Mrs. Bumper was on the job, she slapped Rosebud across the face for spilling some flour on the floor. After that, Rosebud tried to keep out of her reach. But Mrs. Bumper wasn't about to be outsmarted by a snippy black girl; she came armed with a long, green switch from an ash tree. Any time

Mrs. Bumper thought Rosebud was working too slow or being too messy, she switched her across her bare legs, bringing quick tears to Rosebud's eyes.

Rosebud tried not to complain to her pappy, who seemed moody and sad. They talked little at night, too tired to do much else except lie down on their straw mattresses and stare into the shadows. But one night, aching with loneliness for Isaac and her mammy, Rosebud spoke in the darkness.

"Pappy, I disobeyed you the night Isaac was tied up in the stable . . ."

"I know you did, Rosey."

What? Pappy knew?

"It was wrong to disobey me . . . but I didn't have the heart to scold you, knowing you were a comfort to Isaac."

Rosebud's courage rose. "He said something, Pappy. He said, 'Don't worry 'bout me. I don't care what they do. . . . someday I'm gonna be free.' "

There was silence in the cabin. When Abe finally spoke, his voice was choked. "The boy's right. Someday he's gonna be free; I know it." Then her pappy's voice became almost fierce. "And me . . . and you, too. I ain't gonna rest until every Jackson is free."

Abe's words frightened Rosebud. Was her pappy going to run away, too? The thought was terrifying. She didn't want to see her pappy whipped and sold to the chain gang, too.

As the May days got longer, the field hands stayed out in the fields later and later. One evening after work, while waiting for her pappy to come home for supper, Rosebud was pulling weeds in the little garden plot behind the cabin. Her legs still stung from the switching Mrs. Bumper had given her for spilling the chicken gumbo she'd been carrying to the Big House. As she jerked a stubborn weed out by its roots, she muttered, "Why'd you have to run away and get caught, Isaac? Nothin's right anymore, an' it's all your fault!"

As she worked alone in the sweet-smelling earth, she became aware of the voices of two slave women who were also waiting for their men, working in a garden plot just around the corner of the Jackson cabin.

"Some say it's 'bout time for Moses to show up again," said one voice.

"What d'you mean?"

"Ain't you heard? Last couple years, right around seedtime and again around harvest, a few slaves here, a few slaves there, just up and disappear. Ain't never heard from again."

"So? Maybe they got caught and sent down South in a chain gang, just like Abe's boy, Isaac."

"Nah. You always hear about the ones that get caught. Massa Powers makes sure o' that!" The two women laughed. "But the ones that don't get caught . . . they say it's this new Moses who gets 'em out."

"What Moses? Nat Turner's ghost?" Another chuckle.

"Nah. Nobody knows who he is. He ain't violent. But white folks are scared of him just the same— with good reason. They say he can see in the dark like a mule and smell danger down wind like a fox. No one ever hears him comin' 'cause he can move through the underbrush without making a sound— like a tiny fieldmouse. And when he comes, slaves disappear, and no one ever finds 'em."

"True enough?"

Rosebud wanted to hear more, but the field hands were coming back, their weary voices singing to keep their spirits up: "Keep yo' han' on the plow, hold on! . . . If you wanna get to Heaven, let me tell you how . . . Jus' keep yo' han' on de gospel plow . . ."

A short while later Abe watched his daughter in tired silence as she prepared their late supper. Rosebud still wore a tow-linen shirt that hung straight from her shoulders, the same as worn by all slave children. But at age twelve, it only hung to her thighs, showing her long, bare legs.

As she bent over in the dim firelight, Abe suddenly spoke. "Rosebud . . . what are those bruises on your legs?"

Rosebud was startled. "Uh . . . ain't nothing, Pappy."

But Abe got up and turned his daughter so he could see her legs in the flickering firelight. Dozens of switch marks laced the backs of her legs.

"Who's been whippin' you?" he demanded. "That Bumper woman?"

Rosebud nodded, afraid she was going to cry.

Abe swore and slammed a fist into his other hand. Then he sank down on a stool and put his head in his hands. "Sorry, Rosey," he groaned. "Your mammy would roll over in her grave if she heard me talk like that. But I get so mad . . . can't even protect my own children."

Rosebud quickly served up the beans flavored with smoked pork neckbones. She even had a surprise: a couple pieces of sweet potato pie one of the other slave families had given them. But Abe didn't seem to notice.

"Pappy?" Rosebud said, trying to be cheerful. "Tomorrow's Sunday. Ain't no work till Monday. You can rest all day."

"What about you?" he sighed. "They got you up in the cookhouse on Sunday, too?"

"Well . . . just for a while. We made all the food today, but Phoebe and I gotta bring it up to the house for the noon meal when the massa and mistress get back from church goin'. Oughta be okay—Mrs. Bumper's stayin' home tomorrow." Rosebud managed a grin.

Suddenly Abe grabbed Rosebud in a big bear hug. "I'm so sorry, Baby," he said. "Life is tough for you right now. An' I don't know when it's gonna get better. But hang on . . . hang on. One o' these days Moses is gonna come, and then we gonna be free . . ."

"Hush, Pappy," Rosebud shushed him, just like her mother used to do. "You know Mammy didn't like you talkin' 'bout Moses; it's too dangerous. Ever'thing gonna be okay. We got each other."

When Rosebud finally lay down on her straw mattress, she could almost still feel her pappy's arms around her. She felt comforted. At least they had each other. . . .

Rosebud awoke with a start. It was still pitch black inside the cabin. What had awakened her?

Then she heard a strange sound . . . like someone singing right on the other side of the cabin wall. She strained her ears . . . there it was again. The voice was husky and low, one she'd never heard before. Now she could even make out the words.

Go down . . . Moses,
Way down in Egypt land!
Tell old . . . Pharoah,
Let my people go!

That was the song the slaves weren't supposed to sing! Who was singing it? And why was he singing in the middle of the night?

Then Rosebud realized that her pappy had heard the sound, too. He bolted out of bed and stood, half-awake and swaying, in the middle of the dirt floor.

"He's come!" Abe whispered. "Moses has come. We gotta go! We gotta go *now*!"

"What are you sayin', Pappy?" Rosebud cried. "We can't go nowhere! The slave catcher will find us . . . and then . . . and then . . ."

By now Abe was wide awake. "No, don't you see? Tomorrow's Sunday. Ain't nobody gonna miss us for a whole day! And by that time, we will be long gone. 'Cause Moses knows the way, knows where that underground railroad is."

Rosebud watched, frightened, as Abe stole quietly over to the door and opened it a crack. "Come on, now, Rosey. Time has come to go."

Obediently, Rosebud got up, quickly pulled on a

loose jumper over the tow-linen shirt she'd slept in, and started for the door. Then she had a horrible thought.

"Pappy! I can't go. I gotta bring the Powers' dinner to the Big House by midday. If I don't show up, they're gonna know we're gone . . ."

Just then they heard the low, husky voice behind the cabin once more:

Tell old . . . Pharoah,
Let my people go!

Abe seemed frozen to the spot, anguish on his face.

Almost without thinking, Rosebud whispered desperately, "You gotta go, Pappy! You gotta go without me. It's the only way."

Her words shook Abe out of his daze. He grabbed her by the shoulders and looked intensely into her face.

"I'm a-goin', Rosebud. But when I know the way, when I find that underground railroad, I'm comin' back for you. Be ready when harvest is over. Just listen for the whippoorwill."

"Pappy—wait! What do you mean? Whippoor-wills call all the time!"

"No, listen for a code: one time . . . then two times together."

"One time . . . then two times together," Rosebud repeated numbly.

Abe slipped into the night and Rosebud stood trembling in the darkness. Her pappy was gone.

She was all alone.

Chapter 5

Listen for the Whippoorwill

ROSEBUD COULD HARDLY keep her hands from shaking as she and Phoebe carried the cold fried chicken, pickled beets, and a tart made from dried fruit to the back door of the Big House for their Sunday dinner.

"I *said* . . . we forgot the biscuits," repeated Phoebe impatiently. "What's the matter with you? Do I have to say everything twice?"

"Sorry," Rosebud mumbled, and ran back to the cookhouse to get the pan of biscuits. She felt like everyone could tell just by looking at her that her pappy had run away, as if it were written all over her face.

But no one paid any attention to Rosebud. She stayed inside the cabin most of the afternoon, even though the May sunshine was warm and inviting. But that night she hardly slept at all. *Massa gonna find out tomorrow that Pappy is gone,* she thought, her teeth chattering.

Rosebud was at the cookhouse early Monday morning. By the time Mrs. Bumper and Phoebe arrived, she had the fire going in the fireplace and a pot of grits was bubbling gently on an iron hook. Mrs. Bumper looked at her suspiciously, tied on her apron, and set to work.

The women were just getting ready to take breakfast up to the Big House when they heard a horse gallop furiously into the stable yard, then excited voices.

"What's that overseer all hot about?" Phoebe wondered aloud, peeking out the door. "Hey! He's comin' this way!"

The overseer of the field hands, a burly, ugly man with tiny eyes, burst into the cookhouse. "Where is she—Abe Jackson's brat?" he demanded. Then he saw Rosebud. "There you are, you snake!" He grabbed her by the arm, pulled her roughly outside the cookhouse, and pushed her down in the dirt. Then he stood over her threateningly.

"Where's your pappy?" he growled. "Tell me now!"

Rosebud was so frightened that she couldn't speak.

"Ain't gonna talk, eh? I'll loosen your tongue!" With that, the overseer pulled a short leather whip out of his belt and drew back his arm. Instinctively Rosebud put her arms over her head and cringed on the ground, so that the blows fell once, twice on her back.

"What's going on here!" It was Mr. Powers' voice.

The overseer stepped back, his face red and puffing. "It's Abe Jackson, Mr. Powers—he's missing. Didn't turn up at the field this mornin'. Then I found out none of the slaves have seen him since Saturday night. Checked his cabin—it's empty. Thought his kid could tell us somethin'."

Mr. Powers yanked Rosebud to her feet and held her arm tightly. Tears traced small muddy lines down the girl's face and her chest was heaving; she looked down at her bare toes, not daring to look at his face.

"Where's your pappy, girl? Tell me what you know!" her master demanded.

Rosebud shook her head. "I don't know where he is! When I woke up Sunday mornin', he was just gone."

Mr. Powers swore under his breath. "I never thought Abe Jackson would betray me . . . and leave his kid an orphan, to boot." He let go of Rosebud's arm and she stumbled backward.

Mr. Powers whirled on the overseer. "Ride into town. Get as many men to ride with me as possible—tell them there's a reward," he ordered. "Get the sheriff's dogs if you can and meet me back here in an hour. Abe's already got a day's start—but no runaway slave is going to make a fool out of me!" He turned to the white cook who was standing, hands on hips, in the cookhouse doorway. "You—Mrs.

Bumper—pack some food for the saddlebags. And don't let this girl out of your sight."

Within an hour the overseer had returned with three men on horseback and two fierce, slobbering dogs. They took the dogs to the Jackson cabin and let them sniff around, and immediately the dogs took off baying, following the day-old scent into the woods. Mr. Powers and the small posse followed, leaving the overseer in charge of the plantation.

Mrs. Bumper seemed to take an evil pleasure in being given charge of Rosebud. She used the green switch frequently, as if Abe's running away and Mr. Powers' absence gave her permission to punish the girl whenever she wanted.

By day's end, the men and dogs had not returned. When Mrs. Bumper left for the night, the overseer locked Rosebud in her cabin, then let her out the next morning.

Tuesday passed; still no word. Rosebud was so anxious she could hardly eat and only slept out of exhaustion. Then Wednesday a rider came up the front lane toward the Big House. Rosebud's heart beat hopefully. It was Mr. Powers . . . alone.

Without a word the master dismounted and handed the reins of his horse to the stable man, who led the tired animal into the stable. Later that evening Old Jim the butler told a housemaid—who told Phoebe, who whispered to Rosebud—that he overheard Mr. Powers say that the dogs had tracked Abe all the way to the Choptank River, and then all traces of him had disappeared. The dogs went up one side of the river and down the other, and still couldn't find a scent.

"But Massa's gonna put out a wanted poster with a reward," Phoebe reported, shaking her head. "Even if Abe makes it up North, the Fugitive Slave Law makes it possible for someone to catch him and send him back."

Rosebud's hopes sank. Would she ever know if her pappy had made it to freedom?

Gradually the stabs of fear and loneliness that marked Rosebud's days and nights settled into a dull ache. Mr. Powers moved Phoebe into the Jackson cabin with Rosebud, the overseer stopped locking the door at night, and life on the plantation returned to its normal hum of summer work.

Mrs. Bumper was still grouchy and used a switch on Rosebud's legs from time to time, though Rosebud—who was learning to work fast and rarely spilled or made a mess—gave her little reason. But one night after a painful switching, as Rosebud lay on her straw mattress in the hot cabin, straining to hear the night birds over Phoebe's heavy breathing, the girl realized her birthday must have passed. Her mammy had told her she was born in early summer in the prettiest time of the year, when the rosebuds were popping out on the wild rose bushes that splashed color along the edges of the woods.

I'm thirteen years old now, thought Rosebud. *Ain't*

got no mammy . . . ain't got no pappy. That means I'm the woman of the family now. It's time that Mrs. Bumper woman stopped treating me like a naughty child.

Early the next morning before work, Rosebud hurried to the weaving shop with a cloth bundle under her arm. Using a pair of scissors, she cut a few inches off the bottom of her mother's old dress, which Rosebud had washed and put away, then quickly stitched a hem. The dress was still pretty roomy on the slender girl, so she tied it around her waist with

the strip of material she had cut off.

When she arrived at the cookhouse, Rosebud had tucked every piece of her hair under the blue bandana her mother used to wear, just like Phoebe and all the other slave women, and her bare legs were covered to the ankle.

Mrs. Bumper sneered. "Well, ain't you puttin' on airs."

"Ain't puttin' on airs, Miz Bumper," Rosebud said. "But I'm doin' a grown woman's work, and I aim to be treated like one."

Phoebe giggled and, when Mrs. Bumper wasn't looking, winked her approval at Rosebud.

Mrs. Bumper still yelled at Phoebe and Rosebud, just to make herself feel superior, but she no longer tried to switch Rosebud's legs through the long, heavy skirt, knowing it would be useless.

One day in early August, just before the field hands started the first harvest, Mr. Powers called Rosebud to come out of the cookhouse. She went outside, heart thumping. Was it something to do with Pappy? A white man she didn't know was standing with Mr. Powers, dressed in a plain black coat and trousers tucked into riding boots.

"Rosebud, Mr. Jenkins is the blacksmith in town and his wife is about to have another baby. He wants to hire a young girl for a while to do some cooking and cleaning. I'm hiring you out for a spell."

Rosebud almost smiled. Well! She wouldn't mind getting away from Mrs. Bumper. Then, just as suddenly, her spirits fell. What if Pappy came back for her while she was gone? He wouldn't know where she was! He would go away without her!

But Mr. Powers gave her no time to think. "Get your things. You're leaving with Mr. Jenkins right now."

A short time later, Rosebud was sitting on the back of Mr. Jenkins' wagon as it rumbled down the lane. She held a change of clothes and watched the Big House disappear behind the trees.

Rosebud had never been anywhere except the Powers' Plantation, and most of that had been spent in the cookhouse. It was hard to get used to a house on the edge of town, with only one hired man helping Mr. Jenkins in the blacksmith shop. She slept on a pallet in the corner of the kitchen and cooked for the first time in her life on a new-fangled black iron stove.

Mrs. Jenkins seemed frazzled taking care of her two little ones, with another due in a matter of days. She basically left Rosebud to figure out what to do with the cooking, and seemed almost grateful to have something—anything—on the table at meal-time.

The baby was born in the middle of the night. Mr. Jenkins went for the doctor, and Rosebud, lying on her pallet in the kitchen, soon heard a lusty cry from the Jenkins' bedroom. Suddenly, a big dam of sorrow and loneliness seemed to burst inside Rosebud.

If only baby Matthew had lived! How she would have loved to help take care of a new little brother, carting him around on her hip, letting him suck a piece of pork rind when his teeth came in.

If only her mammy hadn't died! Now she had no one to sing the sweet Jesus songs at night, or tell her Bible stories, or just be there with her comforting presence.

If only Isaac hadn't been sold down South in a chain gang! Now she had no friend to catch crawdads in the creek with, or show her how to creep through the woods without frightening the woodland animals. She didn't even have the comfort of her memories, because thinking about Isaac brought looming fears of what his life might be like on the chain gang.

If only Pappy hadn't left her! Now she was alone . . . so alone, with no one who really loved her or cared about her. And now, if he came back, she wouldn't be there, and she'd be alone forever.

The sobs that welled up from deep inside seemed like they were going to tear her apart. Rosebud stuffed a wad of her nightdress into her mouth and cried silently until, exhausted, she fell asleep.

Rosebud had been with the Jenkins only three weeks when a messenger came from the Powers Plantation: Mrs. Powers wanted Rosebud to return. Bewildered, Rosebud gathered up her little bundle and climbed up on the wagon seat beside the old slave who had been sent to fetch her.

"Heh, heh," the man chuckled as they drove out of town. "Miz Powers ain't happy with Mrs. Bumper's cookin' after all. Once you left, she realized you're the only one who really knows how to cook like your mammy."

Rosebud let herself smile real big. She was going home—home where Pappy could find her.

The hot, steamy days of August on the Eastern Shore of Maryland melted into a hot September. All the days seemed alike: sweating in the cookhouse all day long, coming back to the slave quarters to pick vegetables from the little garden plots as twilight fell, then lying in the dark, airless cabin, listening to Phoebe's gentle snores, straining to hear the whippoorwill.

Rosebud heard whippoorwills, all right, along with the *gobble, gobble* of wild turkeys, the twittering of songbirds getting up before sunrise, and the *cut-cut-cut* of the woodcocks. But never anything that sounded like the code her father had given her. As the days gradually turned cooler, Rosebud began to worry. Had she heard it and not recognized it? Had her pappy come and gone?

The harvest was in and cornshucking had begun. On the first day of October, "issue day," Mr. Powers and the overseer handed out new clothes for the coming year. The slave children each received two tow-linen shirts, which they changed once a week. The women were given one dress (to add to last year's), two sets of underthings, and a shawl. The men were given two pairs of trousers, two shirts, and a wool jacket. Everyone was given one pair of shoes, one pair of stockings, and one blanket.

Rosebud felt a sense of pride as she took her things into the cabin. It was the first time she'd been given a dress on issue day, one that fit her a little better than the one she'd cut down from her mammy. She tried on the shoes, but they hurt so bad she took them off again.

Instead of spreading out the new blanket over her straw mattress, Rosebud rolled up her new dress and shawl in the blanket and tied it with the strip of cloth she'd cut off her mother's old dress—just in case. She wanted to have her best clothing ready to go if the signal came in the night. Then, using the blanket roll as a pillow, Rosebud fell into a contented sleep.

She awoke with a start. What had awakened her? She listened. But all she heard was Phoebe's steady breathing and an occasional snore.

Then suddenly she heard it. *Whip-poor-will* . . . Silence. Then, *whip-poor-will, whip-poor-will.*

Rosebud's heart seemed to beat in her throat. One time, then two times together. That was it! The code!

She scrambled to her feet and grabbed the bedroll she'd been using for a pillow. Creeping over to the fireplace, she felt around until she found last night's pan of cold corn bread and smoked fish, rolled them in one of her mother's old bandanas, and tucked it in her belt.

She listened. All was silent. Had she heard right? What if it wasn't Pappy after all? What if it was just an old whippoorwill grubbing for insects . . . ?

Whip-poor-will . . . Silence. *Whip-poor-will, whip-poor-will.*

There it was again! Now she had no doubts. Holding her breath, she quietly opened the cabin door and slipped into the night.

Chapter 6

A Friend with Friends

A S SHE SHUT THE DOOR of the cabin behind her, Rosebud stopped. Which direction had the sound come from? *Oh, Jesus . . . let it come again.* She waited, hardly daring to breathe.

Then she heard it once more. One bird call . . . then two, coming from the direction of the creek. Quickly Rosebud ran through the trees, swinging wide so that she didn't come too close to the stable, hardly noticing the rocks and sticks she stepped on with her bare feet in the dark.

As she came near to the creek, Rosebud slowed to a walk. Where was Pappy? She kept walking, looking this way and that in the darkness, but seeing nothing.

Then suddenly a low, husky voice called quietly:

"Over here." Slowly Rosebud followed the voice behind a thick clump of ash trees. She could see a shadow, a shape . . . who was it? The girl stood still.

"Pappy?" she whispered.

"Shhh," said the husky voice. "Come."

It wasn't her father's voice! For a panicked moment, Rosebud wondered whether to run back to the safety of the cabin. But her feet started to walk after the dark shape ahead of her. As her eyes adjusted to the moonless night, hidden beneath low October clouds, Rosebud realized that the person in front of her was not wearing trousers, but a skirt.

Was this woman taking her to her pappy? There was only one way to find out. Rosebud kept walking, clutching her bundle close to her chest.

They'd been walking through the woods about half an hour without speaking a word when a small clearing suddenly opened up in front of them. Other dark shapes moved . . . more people. Her eyes made out two men and two more women.

One of the men moved toward Rosebud and her guide. She knew immediately it wasn't her pappy; his shape was too tall, too skinny.

"Who you got with you?" the man demanded in a whisper. He peered closely at Rosebud. "What? This ain't nothing but a young'un—a girl at that!" The man swore. "How she gonna keep up? An' we already have a babe in arms. . . . How we gonna keep it from cryin' and givin' us all away?"

Rosebud's heart beat faster. Was this the man they called Moses? What if he wouldn't let her go with them?

"Where's my pappy . . . Abe Jackson?" she managed to ask, pushing the words past the lump in her throat.

"Your pappy ain't here," whispered the woman who had guided her through the woods. "He wanted to come for you, but it wasn't safe. We gonna take you to him if we can."

Conflicting emotions collided inside Rosebud. She wanted to cry with disappointment that her pappy hadn't come. But . . . he must be alive! She wanted to cry out, *Is he well? Is he free?*

But the low, husky voice commanded: "Come on, now. We gotta make tracks before mornin' light."

The woman took off quickly through the woods, with the little group keeping up as best they could. Rosebud, not wanting to get lost, followed close to their guide. Behind her came the other two women; one was carrying a bundle that might be the baby the man mentioned. The two men brought up the rear.

Rosebud was bewildered. *What is going on here? Is that tall, skinny man the "Moses" that Pappy had talked about? But why is the woman leading the way?*

After a while Rosebud noticed something else. The woman in front of her moved almost silently through the woods, while the group behind her crashed and stumbled in the dark. Rosebud tried to remember what Isaac had said about walking quietly in the woods: avoid stepping on dry leaves and sticks that might snap . . . walk on spongy moss or

hard dirt to avoid leaving a trail . . . don't make any sudden movements. But he hadn't told her how to do that in the dark!

The blanket roll she carried seemed to get heavier and heavier. A couple of times Rosebud's eyes flew open and her head jerked as if she'd fallen asleep for a few seconds while plodding through the night.

Then suddenly, the woman stopped and held up her hand. The followers listened. All Rosebud could hear was the gentle sound of water swishing and splashing, like the creek behind the stable back home.

"Into the water," the woman commanded. "Best way to cover our scent. Follow exactly where I go." Before anyone could protest, she pulled up the bottom of her skirt, tucked it in her belt, and stepped down a small, muddy bank into the dark water.

Following her example, Rosebud tucked the bottom of her dress into her belt. The mud squished between Rosebud's toes and felt soothing to her sore feet. The water was cold, but only came up to her knees and she soon got used to it.

Rosebud couldn't tell how long they walked in the creek. It was slow going. The creek's bottom was full of smooth, slippery rocks, and it took all her concentration not to fall into the water. Then she became aware of a new sound: the muffled cries of a baby waking from sleep.

Finally, their guide climbed out of the water and sat down on the ground. Gratefully Rosebud sank down on the grassy bank and leaned against a tree.

The woman with the baby sat down close-by, unbuttoned the top of her dress, and put the fussing baby to nurse. The second man touched her gently on the shoulder before sitting down and resting his arms and his head on his knees.

That's when Rosebud realized the people around her were no longer just dark shapes, but she could make out their features and clothes. She looked up through the trees; the sky was getting lighter in the east.

The woman with the baby looked just a little older than Phoebe. Was the young man who touched her her husband? The other woman was a little older and stouter, but not fat. Then there was the tall, skinny man who seemed to have a permanent scowl on his face.

After a curious glance around the little group, Rosebud's gaze rested on the woman who had guided them through the night. She had a plain face, framed by a bandana tied neatly around her head. The most outstanding thing about her was an ugly scar, right in the middle of her forehead.

The woman stood up. For the first time, Rosebud realized how short she was. With no trouble at all, Rosebud could look her right in the eye.

"It's time to go," the woman said in her peculiar, husky voice. "Everyone must be very quiet and move slowly. We are almost to our first station."

Station? Rosebud thought, as the little group got up wearily and began to move again. *Does she mean a train station?* Her heartbeat quickened. Maybe they were going to ride on the strange railroad her pappy had told her about, the one that went underground.

As dawn approached, the trees began to thin out. They were coming to the edge of the woods. The short woman stopped and held up her hand for absolute silence. Then Rosebud saw something strange through the bushes: a lantern, burning brightly, was hanging from a fencepost. And be-

yond the lantern stood a small white farmhouse.

Whose farm is this? Rosebud wondered. It didn't look anything like the Powers Plantation! Maybe it belonged to some free Negroes, farming for themselves. *Oh, how Pappy would love to have a little farm for himself and his own family....*

Her thoughts were interrupted as their guide motioned the little group to follow her quickly through the gate and up the wide path to the farmhouse door. The woman's eyes darted to the right and to the left, watching, listening.

At the door the woman gave a knock. Two knocks, then three together. It seemed like an eternity before a muffled voice on the other side of the door said, "Who's there?"

"A friend with friends," said the husky voice softly.

The door opened a crack, then wider.

Rosebud's eyes widened. It was a white woman! They'd been tricked!

Chapter 7

Follow the River

ROSEBUD WAS TERRIFIED. They were all going to get caught—just like Isaac had been! She turned to run but the little black woman with the scar grabbed her wrist in a steel-like grip and pulled her into the doorway.

"Come in quickly," whispered the white woman, who was wearing a long nightdress, her hair tucked up under a ruffled nightcap. "One, two, three . . . six passengers," she counted. "And a baby . . . my, my." She led the way down a short hall to a door, which she opened.

Steep, narrow stairs led down to a cellar. With her wrist still held in the steel-like grip, Rosebud felt herself being pulled down the stairs, the others following close behind. It was dark in the cellar, but soon a lantern was handed down the stairs. Then Rosebud heard the sound of a key turning in a lock.

"Oh, no!" Rosebud cried in a panic. "We're prisoners now! The slave catcher's gonna get us! Mr. Powers's gonna sell me to the chain gang for sure—"

"Hush, girl!" commanded the husky voice. "We're safe here—if you don't make a racket and wake up the whole countryside."

Rosebud choked off her words, but her heart was still racing. What was happening? Who were these white people? Why had they been locked in the cellar?

The stout woman came over to Rosebud and wrapped her big arms around the girl. "There, there, child. Don't be frightened. It's been a hard night. Sure you're scared—we all are. But it's all right. There, there . . ."

Gradually Rosebud relaxed in the woman's warm embrace. For just a moment, it felt like she was safe in her mammy's arms again.

Then the woman nodded her head in the direction of the woman with the scar. "Don't you know who this is, honey?" she whispered.

Rosebud shook her head.

"Why, this here is the one black folks call 'Moses,' 'cause she's been leadin' folks like us out of slavery to freedom . . . but most white people call her a slave stealer." The stout woman chuckled. "Whatever they call her, I heard that she can put a hex on a mad dog, an'—"

"—see in the dark like a mule, and creep silently

through the forest like a fieldmouse," giggled Rosebud.

"Nonsense!" the husky voice snorted, overhearing their whispered conversation. "I'm only a woman who listens to the good Lord and lets Him lead me wherever He wants me to go. My name is Harriet Tubman, child. You can call me Harriet—I was named after my mammy."

So 'Moses' was a woman, not a man! Rosebud felt ashamed of her fears. This small woman, no bigger than she was, had braved the dangers of being a runaway—not once, but again and again! "But . . . if you're the one they call Moses," Rosebud stammered, "did you take my pappy on the . . . the . . ."

"Underground railroad?" Harriet Tubman smiled. "Yes, I did. Abe Jackson traveled with me last spring."

"Where is he? Is he all right? Is he free? When can I . . .?" The words tumbled out in a rush.

But Harriet signaled with her hand for silence. The key was turning in the lock at the top of the cellar stairs. Then a white man came down the stairs.

Rosebud instinctively lowered her eyes as she'd been taught to do in the presence of a white man. Then she heard the man say, "I brought you breakfast. Eat all you want. You're going to need your strength."

Rosebud lifted her head. The man was setting down a bucket of fresh, warm milk with a dipper in it and a basket with rolls, butter, and cold sausage.

Hands reached for the food, but Harriet stopped

them. "Lord God Almighty," she prayed, her eyes squeezed tight and her hands raised toward heaven, "thank You for Your bountiful blessing—"

"Amen!" the tall, skinny man interrupted and grabbed a sausage.

While they ate, Rosebud found out the names of the others. The stout woman was Mary Tucker, and the young woman with the baby was her sister Sally. The young man was Sally's husband, Tobias Brown, and their baby boy was named Toby after his pappy. Mary, Sally, and Tobias were from a plantation near Bucktown. The tall, skinny man's name was Charles Walker, and he had run away from a plantation over by Church Creek.

"Who are these white folks?" asked Charles nervously, jerking his head toward the footsteps overhead. "An' when are we gonna get on that train that travels underground?"

Harriet Tubman shook her head. "Don't ask names. If any of us get caught, they can't make us tell somethin' we don't know." Then her eyes twinkled. "But just to set your mind at ease, I've stopped at this station on the 'underground railroad' more times than I can count—and I ain't never lost a passenger yet."

Rosebud was puzzled. If this farmhouse was a station on the underground railroad, where was the train? She was just about to ask when Harriet lay down on the cellar floor, using a sack of potatoes for a pillow.

"Better get some sleep," grunted the small woman. "We won't be movin' before nightfall."

Rosebud yawned. She *was* tired from all that walking, and her tummy was full. Rosebud laid her head on her bedroll, listening to the contented gurgles of baby Toby . . .

"Wake up, girl!"

Rosebud opened her eyes. The room was dark. What was that strange voice? Where was she?

Then it all came back to her in a rush: she had run away, and she had no idea where she was.

"It's our turn to use the privy." The voice belonged to Mary Tucker. "Then the white lady says we gotta be ready to go."

Groggily, Rosebud followed Mary up the cellar steps, then out the back door of the farmhouse to a small outhouse. It was already dark, but there were no clouds. A few stars were starting to twinkle.

When they arrived back in the cellar, a lantern had been lit. Mary and Rosebud joined the others who were dipping something hot and steaming out of a big bowl onto pretty plates with blue flowers. Rosebud stared. Whoever heard of a white woman letting slaves eat off her china plates! She took a bite of the strange food—sliced potatoes in some kind of creamy sauce. Rosebud thought she had never tasted anything so good.

Then it was time to go. The farm lady gave each person a roll left over from breakfast and a hunk of cheese to take along. One by one the runaways slipped out the back door to the barn. Two farm horses were harnessed to a wagon inside. Without a word, the farmer helped each person lie down in the wagon bed and covered them with rough potato sacks. Rosebud heard a gentle sucking sound and realized that Sally Brown must be trying to nurse the baby to sleep so it wouldn't make any noise.

With a jerk, the wagon rolled out of the barn. The wagon bed was hard and uncomfortable, and the potato sacks made Rosebud itch. The road was bumpy, jostling the bodies under the sacks back and forth. Rosebud lost all track of time, but at one point it sounded like the wagon rolled over a bridge.

After a long time—was it one hour? two hours?—they heard the farmer say, "Whoa . . . whoa." The wagon stopped. Then they heard, "It's all right; you can get out now."

Gratefully, Rosebud pushed off the potato sacks and crawled stiffly out of the wagon. She saw the farmer talking to Harriet Tubman.

"Head straight through those woods, Mrs. Tubman, and you'll get to the Choptank River. Just follow the river—it'll eventually take you to Camden, Delaware. From there . . . well, you know the way to Philadelphia from Camden."

Mrs. Tubman? What a strange white man. Rosebud had never heard white people call black people by anything but their first name—or "girl," or "boy," or "hey, you."

The little black woman and the burly white farmer shook hands, then the little group headed into the woods. Behind them they heard the farmer say quietly: "God go with you."

Once again the little group walked all through the night. Rosebud could see the Choptank River through the trees. It was a big river—nothing like the little creek running through the Powers Plantation. From time to time, Harriet waded into the river and walked along the shallow water next to the shore to hide their scent just in case someone sent dogs after them.

As the night wore on, Rosebud began to tire and dropped back little by little. Once she looked up, and the others had disappeared. Frightened she started to run, but the others were just beyond the next clump of trees.

"See?" grumbled Charles. "The young'un won't be able to keep up; gonna slow us all down."

"You walk first, Mr. Walker," said Harriet. "Just keep the river in sight. We'll all be right behind."

Charles Walker grunted in agreement and moved on, his long legs setting a faster pace. Tobias put his arm around his wife's waist and helped her along. Mary was taking a turn carrying the sleeping baby. Harriet brought up the rear with Rosebud. To Rosebud's surprise, the woman began to talk to her.

"How old are you, Rosebud . . . thirteen? I remember when I was thirteen. Can't never forget, 'cause that year changed my whole life."

Rosebud forgot about being tired. She could hardly imagine that this daring woman had ever been a young girl like herself.

"It was cornhusking time on the Brodas Plantation—that's where I grew up, down near Bucktown. We were workin' fast, people were singin' and havin' a good time. But I saw one of the field hands who was keepin' to himself, lookin' around now and then. So I watched him. Suddenly, when the overseer wasn't lookin', he up and starts runnin'. Well, it didn't take long for the overseer to realize he was missin' and go off after him. I was a curious child, so I followed along behind to see what was gonna happen.

"Well, the slave had snuck into a store, hoping to hide. But the overseer went into the store and I followed, lookin' in the doorway. Just then the slave made a run for it. The overseer was standin' by the counter, askin' the storekeeper if he'd seen his slave, when he heard the commotion. Seeing his slave just about to get away, he grabbed a heavy weight from the counter and threw it with all his might toward the door. I saw it comin' but I just stood there . . . and that's the last thing I remembered for weeks on end."

"Is that how you got that scar?"

"Sure enough. I nearly died, and it took months before I could get out of bed and able to work again. I often heard my mammy prayin', 'Lord, I'm holdin' steady on to You and You've got to see us through.' And sure enough, He did. And," the woman chuckled softly, "as far as I know, that slave got clean away. God sure works in mysterious ways."

Mysterious ways is right, thought Rosebud. Sometimes she couldn't figure out if God was for her or against her. Her brother didn't get away . . . and her mammy and baby brother died. Rosebud shook those upsetting thoughts out of her head. Right now she could at least be thankful that her pappy had gotten to freedom, and that she had heard the "whippoorwill" and found Harriet Tubman.

As the sky began to lighten, Harriet called the group to a stop. "There's no station near here—we're goin' to have to lie low during the day. Can't risk walkin'." With that, Harriet plunged deeper into the woods, away from the river. She halted where the underbrush was thick, almost impassable.

"Find yourself a thicket to hide in. Try to get some sleep if possible. We'll walk again when darkness can cover us."

Walking had kept Rosebud fairly warm during the cool night, but once they stopped she began to shiver. Then she remembered her new shawl. Unrolling her bundle, she put on her new dress over the old one, wrapped herself in her shawl, and lay down on the blanket. Within moments she was fast asleep.

That night the little group set out again, following the same pattern: walking in the woods for a while, then wading in the river. Rosebud ate the corn bread and smoked fish she'd brought from home. Afterwards she was still hungry and was tempted to eat the bread and cheese, but decided to wait.

About midnight, Rosebud noticed that Harriet was leading them away from the river. Soon they came to a road. Harriet still kept to the woods, keeping the road in sight, until they saw the few scattered buildings of a small town.

"What's this?" demanded Charles.

"Our next station," said Harriet. Walking swiftly, she approached the back door of a house that was a little separated from the others and knocked.

There was no answer.

Harriet knocked again and waited. Finally a muffled voice said, "Who is it?"

"A friend with friends."

The door cracked open an inch. "Go away! Go now!" The man's voice was urgent. "The slave catchers were here today . . . they searched the entire house. It isn't safe! Go away!" And the door shut in their faces.

Chapter 8

"Move On—or Die!"

WITHOUT A MOMENT'S HESITATION, Harriet plunged back into the woods, the others right at her heels. Rosebud was so tired that she stumbled several times. She felt like she couldn't walk another whole night! But she kept going, putting one foot in front of the other.

"Faster," Harriet urged. Then Rosebud heard her mumble under her breath, "Lord, I'm goin' to hold steady on to You, and You've got to see us through."

The little group headed back toward the Choptank River, but soon the ground began to feel mushy and soft underfoot. The Choptank had large swampy areas spreading out from its banks. Harriet tried to avoid them while staying as far from the road as possible, but the going was slow.

As a new October day began to dawn, baby Toby started to fret. His mother tried to nurse him as she walked, but Toby would have none of it. Soon his fretting had become a loud cry.

"Make that baby shut up!" hissed Charles angrily.

Harriet stopped, fished in the big pockets of her skirt, and pulled out a brown medicine bottle. "Didn't want to use this unless necessary," she said, "but this will help keep the baby quiet."

Sally looked worried, but tried to hold Toby still as Harriet poured some liquid from the brown bottle down his throat.

"What is it?" Rosebud whispered to Mary. She took advantage of the brief stop to unwrap the bread and cheese still in her bandana, then stuff as much as she could into her mouth.

"Probably tincture of opium—a drug that will put him to sleep for a few hours."

"Shh!" Harriet said, holding up her hand for silence. They listened. A dog was barking in the distance. Then it was joined by another . . . and another.

"Into the swamp—*now!*" Harriet commanded, and plunged right into the mud and marshy grasses. Gulping the food in her mouth and clutching her bundle, Rosebud tried to hurry, but the mud seemed to pull at her ankles and hold her back. As she struggled on, the mud turned to swampy water and got deeper. It crept up to her knees, then her thighs, and the bottom of her dress was soaked. But ahead of her, Harriet kept right on pushing. Behind them, the barking dogs seemed to be closing in.

As the swamp got deeper, a layer of fog seemed to be sitting on the surface. Soon Rosebud was chest deep in the marshy water; even the men were wet to the waist. Only little Toby was dry, slung over his pappy's shoulder, fast asleep.

Holding her bundle on her head with one hand, Rosebud pushed aside the tangle of water lilies, float-

ing mossy beds, and tall grasses. Little green frogs leaped for their lives as the two-legged creatures invaded their home.

The barking of the dogs seemed to change to a frenzied hunting bay. Then they heard shouts: "The dogs have picked up a trail! This way!"

Harriet Tubman was pushing through the water

lilies toward a little grove of skinny trees sticking up out of the fog. "Get down—as far as you can get," she hissed as they all squeezed in among the trees and grasses.

Rosebud lowered herself in the marshy water up to her neck, knowing it was useless trying to keep her bundle dry now. Her heart was pounding and her mouth was dry. *Oh, Jesus, Jesus, don't let them find us!*

Somewhere through the fog they could hear the men and dogs crashing through the woods. Then more shouts: "They've gone into the swamp!"

"You're crazy—they can't hide in the swamp."

"Look at the dogs. They have lost the trail right here at the edge of the swamp."

"Well, they gotta come out somewhere. Come on."

The noises headed upriver and soon faded away. Charles started to rise out of the water, but Harriet put her finger to her lips, frowned, and gave a slight shake of her head. Her meaning was clear: it might be a trick; the slave catchers could have left someone behind.

The sun crept higher in the sky and burned off the layer of fog on the swamp. Flies and other insects started buzzing around their heads. *If only I could have a drink!* Rosebud thought, licking her dry lips. Once she felt a snake slither between her ankles under water, and she had to stifle a scream.

A couple of times Rosebud looked at Harriet and saw that her eyes were closed and her mouth was moving. She could barely hear the almost silent whisper: "Lord, I'm holdin' steady on to You, and You've got to see us through."

Then baby Toby started to stir on his pappy's shoulder. "I need to feed him," whispered Sally, tears in her eyes.

Harriet shook her head. "Can't risk it," she whispered back. Feeling under the water for her pocket, Harriet brought out the brown bottle and gave Toby another dose of the tincture of opium. Soon the baby fell back into his drugged sleep.

Then they heard voices again.

"Hear anything?" said one voice.

"Nah. I don't think they're in there. And I'm getting tired sitting here waiting."

So! The slave catchers *had* left someone behind!

Rosebud wanted to cry. Would they ever get out

of the swamp? What if those men and dogs stayed there all day and all night?

The voices and noises faded away once more. But Harriet shook her head: it still wasn't safe.

Soon the sun was high overhead and the biting insects seemed unbearable. But after a while a shadow passed over the swamp. Clouds were gathering swiftly and Rosebud could feel a breeze off the river. And then it began to rain, an autumn downpour.

Finally Harriet left the little grove of trees and waded back through the swamp under cover of the heavy rain. Gratefully, the others followed, thoroughly soaked to the skin. Rosebud tilted her head up and let the cool, clean rain run into her dry mouth.

Harriet led them back downriver before they came out of the swamp. Rosebud thought she had never in her life been so wet and smelly and miserable. The little group made a camp of sorts in the woods, and when the rain stopped, they stripped off their outer clothing and spread it on the bushes to dry.

Rosebud undid her bundle, wrung out her shawl and blanket, then wrapped them around her. "M-M-Miz Harriet," she said, her teeth chattering, "ain't we ever goin' to ride that underground train?"

Harriet didn't answer. Instead she got a faraway look in her eyes. "Did you ever hear the story of Tice Davids?" She didn't wait for an answer. "Ol' Tice was born a slave, just like you an' me. But one day he sees his chance to run and heads for Ohio—that's a free state out West, you know. Trouble is, his master found out quick-like and was after him like greased lightning. Oh, man, he was hot on Tice Davids' tail, couldn't have been more than five minutes behind.

"Then Ol' Tice comes to the Ohio River; in he goes and swims across. Master comes along behind, sees Tice climbing out the other side, and calls someone to row him across. But when that master got to the other side, he couldn't find a trace of Tice Davids nowhere! He went up the river; he went down the river. 'It's just like he disappeared on an underground road!' the master said when he came back empty-handed." Harriet's eyes were wide and mysterious.

"Well, about that time . . . this was around 1831—I was younger than you, 'bout ten years old—ever'body was talking about them new-fangled steam engine trains. An' pretty soon folks were saying that Tice Davids had disappeared on an *underground railroad*. Well, this gave the abolitionists an idea . . ."

"Abo . . . aboli—what?" said Rosebud.

"Abolitionists. That's what they call folks who think slavery is wrong, and not only think it, but do something about it!"

By this time, Mary, Sally, and Tobias had moved closer so they could hear the story. Even Charles, though his back was turned, seemed to be listening.

"Anyway," Harriet continued, "this gave the abolitionists an idea. The folks who were willing to help runaway slaves started using railroad code words to talk about escape routes. Me, I'm a 'conductor'; you're my 'passengers.' Or sometimes runaways are called 'parcels' or 'bales of black cotton.' Safe houses with secret rooms or haylofts are called 'stations' and the people who run them . . ."

Harriet's eyelids started to sag, and her words suddenly started to slur.

" . . . are called . . . 'station masters' . . ."

Without further warning, Harriet just toppled over and lay crumpled on the ground.

"Oh, Lordy . . ." Mary said, moving swiftly to the small woman's side. Rosebud stared. What was happening?

Tobias knelt down and checked Harriet's pulse. Then he looked at the others.

"I think she's all right; she's just sleeping . . ."

"Sleeping!" snorted Charles. "People don't fall asleep like that!"

"What I mean is," said Tobias patiently, "I heard that sometimes Miz Tubman has sleeping spells—on account of that head injury she had as a young girl. Sometimes she sleeps a couple hours, sometimes a whole day, but she wakes up again, and then she's fine."

Sure enough, Harriet was breathing long, slow breaths, as if she was in a deep sleep.

"You mean we have to wait here till she wakes up?" said Charles. "It's almost nightfall—time to be movin' on. What if those slave catchers come back?"

Tobias stood up and glared at Charles. "Yes, we wait. She's been riskin' her life to help us. The least we can do is stick by her during this spell."

Charles grumbled but sat down again. Rosebud shivered as she pulled the damp shawl and blanket tighter around her against the cool night air. Because of hiding in the swamp all day, she had not slept for twenty-four hours. Even though she was worried about Harriet Tubman, she was grateful to lie down and close her eyes.

"Rosebud. Wake up."

Rosebud sat up with a start. It was Harriet, shaking her, then shaking each of the others in turn. "Come on, it's time to go," the woman whispered huskily.

The night was pitch black; clouds still covered the moon. Rosebud smiled to herself; she was glad Harriet was all right. But . . . her throat hurt. If only she could get a drink!

As the little group got up stiffly and gathered their still damp clothes from the bushes, Harriet said, "I'm sorry my sleeping spell has set us back. I should've warned you, but it's been half a year since I last had a spell. But now we got some fast walkin' to do to make up for lost—"

"Count me out."

It was Charles's voice. All eyes turned and stared at him.

"What do you mean, man?" said Tobias.

"I mean I ain't goin' on. Some 'underground railroad' this is! We ain't got no food . . . we've been sittin' all day in the swamp like drowned rats . . . an' now we find out this little woman here has sleepin' spells. Some Moses you are!"

Charles snatched his damp clothes from the bushes and tied them into a bundle with a piece of rope he wore around his waist. "At least back on the plantation, I had two meals a day and a roof over my head," he muttered, slinging the bundle over his shoulder. "If I turn up on my own account, maybe my master won't take it so hard that I been gone a few days."

In the stillness of the woods, everyone heard the metal click, and then Harriet's low, husky voice: *"No one goes back."*

All eyes turned toward Harriet Tubman. She was standing with her feet apart, arm outstretched, pointing a pistol at Charles's chest.

"I'm not afraid to use this, Charles Walker. You move on with us—or you die!"

Chapter 9

The Funny Parson

T HERE WAS A SHOCKED silence. Then
Charles slowly grinned. "You
wouldn't shoot me . . . a little
woman like you."

The pistol never
wavered. "If you
try to leave,
you're a
dead man."

"But
why?"
Tobias
protested.
"Let him
go. We'll be

better off without him. Rosebud, here, complains less than he does."

Harriet kept the pistol pointed at Charles. "A runaway who turns back is dangerous," she said quietly. "His master or the slave catchers will force him to tell what route we've taken . . . who has helped us along the way . . . where the stations on the underground railroad are. I'll kill one cowardly slave before I'll let him endanger the lives of hundreds of innocent people."

For half a minute, everyone stood frozen. Then Charles set his bundle down. "All right, all right. I'll go on with you. You womenfolk need another man to protect you, anyhow."

Rosebud was tempted to giggle—if her throat hadn't hurt so much. She suspected that in a tight spot, Charles would look out for himself. But Harriet slowly lowered the pistol and said, "That's right. We all need to help each other."

Within a few minutes they were once again moving through the night. Rosebud kept close to Mary, but they walked silently. Her throat hurt too much to talk. As the night wore on, the young girl also realized how hungry she was. She reached for the bandana tucked in her waist with the last of the bread and cheese—it was gone. It must have fallen out in the swamp.

As the birds began greeting the first rays of daylight, Harriet pointed out berries that were safe to eat. Rosebud eagerly picked a handful of huckleberries and put them in her mouth all at once. They were past their prime and had lost their juiciness, but at least they were something to eat. But she had difficulty swallowing them.

As the sky got brighter, the little group hid themselves among the thick underbrush and dropped off to sleep quickly from exhaustion.

In her sleep, Rosebud dreamed that someone was standing with a heavy boot on her chest. She could hardly breathe. Had the slave catcher caught her? What was going to happen to her? Why did he keep standing on her chest? Why couldn't she breathe?

A coughing fit woke her, and she realized she'd been dreaming. There was no one standing on her chest, but it hurt and she found that it was hard to get a deep breath. She squinted at the sun; by its position, Rosebud figured it must be midafternoon— too early to continue their journey along the river. She coughed a couple more times, then lay back on her bed of moss and leaves with her eyes closed, listening to the *chit-chit-chit* of the squirrels and the honking of geese flying south, high overhead. It was so peaceful, it was almost easy to forget that she was hiding in the woods as a runaway.

Suddenly Rosebud had the distinct impression that someone was watching her. Her eyes flew open . . . and she found herself staring into the face of a white boy a little older than herself standing about five feet away.

Immediately the boy put a finger to his lips. "Wake up the others," he whispered. "Thee must come with me—quickly."

Rosebud blinked. It wasn't a dream. The boy was still there, wearing a funny black hat with a flat brim. Again he whispered, "Quickly! Wake up the others."

Frightened, Rosebud scrambled to her feet and woke up Harriet Tubman first, then Mary and the others. Harriet immediately stood up and went over to the boy, who looked about fifteen.

"I have been looking for thee," he said. "Thee must all come with me quickly."

With that the boy turned and started through the woods, heading away from the river.

"Do you know who that boy is?" hissed Charles Walker, frowning suspiciously.

"No, I don't," Harriet admitted. "But he has the speech of the Quakers, many of whom have been our friends. I think we should trust him. But," she looked at each of them, "be watchful."

Rosebud brushed bits of dried leaves and moss from her dress, then had to run to catch up with the others. The boy was walking swiftly and the fast pace made it hard for Rosebud to muffle the coughing that pushed up from her chest. If only she could get a good, deep breath!

They must have walked about half an hour before the boy finally slowed and stopped. The woods opened up onto a small meadow, and in the middle sat a plain, white, one-story building. It did not look like a house or a barn. Four wooden steps led to a door in the front of the building, and four steps led out the back. Along the side were five windows in a row.

The boy stepped into the clearing and looked around the meadow carefully. Then he motioned for the others to follow as he strode quickly toward the building and led them inside.

Just inside the front door Rosebud sank down on a bench and looked around. All she saw were two rows of wooden benches on either side of a large room. What was this—a church? Rosebud had never been inside one before . . . though her mammy used to tell her about the log cabin churches the slaves had, before the white people passed a law saying slaves couldn't go to church or learn to read. Mammy said white folks thought black folks got too many strange ideas from the Bible about being free like everyone else.

"Wait here," said the boy quietly. "Don't stand near the windows. I'll be back." Then he was gone.

"Are we gonna stay here?" said Charles. "This could be a trap."

Harriet was thoughtful. "Tobias, you watch near the windows on that side, and Charles, you watch on the other. Stand so you can't be seen from outside, but be alert."

Sally was stripping off baby Toby's soiled, damp clothes and putting on some fresh ones that she had tucked inside her dress. By now the baby was wide awake and whimpering for his breakfast.

Rosebud's head was pounding so hard that she hardly noticed when Mary sat down on the bench beside her. Mary pulled Rosebud close, so that her head could rest on Mary's big shoulder.

"Someone's comin'," said Tobias in a quiet voice. "It's the boy, and he's got a white man with him."

"Just one?" asked Harriet. Tobias nodded.

The little group stood and faced the back door as the boy came in with the man right behind him. The middle-aged man was dressed similarly to the boy: black trousers and a plain black coat over a white shirt, and a funny looking black hat with a flat brim.

The man looked around from person to person.

"Well, well, well, Isaac," he said, "who has thee found?"

Rosebud's head jerked up. The boy's name was *Isaac*? Just like her brother!

"Who is the leader of this group?" asked the man politely.

Harriet stepped forward. "My name is Harriet Tubman. My friends and I are seeking safe passage to Pennsylvania."

"Harriet Tubman?" asked the man. He stroked his beard thoughtfully. "I have heard of Harriet Tubman—'the Moses of her people,' they say—but I never thought I would have the honor of meeting thee." He held out his hand. "I am Benjamin Woodhouse. My family and I are Quakers. This is our meetinghouse."

"Are you a preacher then?" Mary spoke up.

"No, friend. Quakers don't have preachers. I am the clerk of our meeting, which . . . never mind. That's not really important right now. Art thou hungry?"

Everyone just stared at him.

"What a foolish question," the man chided himself. "Of course thou art hungry. We will bring something to thee shortly. Isaac, run tell thy mother we need food—lots of food." As Isaac ran off, the man then turned back to Harriet. "Friend Harriet, I am afraid this meetinghouse is somewhat bare with only hard benches for thy comfort. But thee must stay here until nightfall. Then thee can come to the house under cover of darkness."

Harriet drew herself up to her full height, which was only five feet. "Sir, are you a station master?"

"A . . . what?"

Rosebud saw the alarm in the others' faces. This man didn't know anything about the "underground railroad." It could be a trap after all!

98

But the man caught their looks. "Wait," he said. "I think I know what thou art asking. No, I am not a station master on . . . what did Friend Thomas call it? . . . the 'underground railroad,' yes. But Friend Thomas—that's Thomas Garret in Philadelphia . . ."

A broad smile broke out on Harriet's plain face. "You know Thomas Garret, the man who makes shoes?"

"Yes, indeed," smiled Benjamin Woodhouse. "It is he who hast told me of you. We—my wife Maggie and I—have been troubled in our spirit for some time because of slavery in the land. But we have felt helpless, not knowing what one small family could do. But I was in Philadelphia on business and stopped to see Friend Thomas, a fellow Quaker, and he—"

"I am sorry I doubted you," Harriet Tubman interrupted. "Thomas Garret is a great friend of the abolitionists, black and white alike. He has risked his life and reputation many times—and his money, too, I understand."

"Yes, yes, thou art quite right," Benjamin chuckled. "He was fined a goodly amount for aiding runaways and breaking the Fugitive Slave Law—an evil law in the sight of God! God help us all."

The small black woman and the Quaker man with the strange speech sat down on a bench and talked on as the others listened or nodded off in sleep. Between coughs, Rosebud heard Harriet say, "Your boy said, 'I've been lookin' for thee.' What did he mean?"

Benjamin shook his head. "Well, that is the

strange thing. He was telling me—ah! Here is Isaac now, and his mother, with thy food."

A pretty, middle-aged white woman in a plain black dress and white cap came in the back door of the Quaker meetinghouse with Isaac, both of them carrying baskets and a steaming iron kettle.

"Maggie, this is Harriet Tubman, of whom Friend Thomas told us so much, and these are . . . these are . . ." Benjamin Woodhouse looked perplexed.

Harriet came to his rescue and briefly introduced each of her "passengers" by name. Rosebud thought the boy Isaac looked at her funny when Mrs. Tubman said her name was Rosebud Jackson. But she soon forgot about it as the iron kettle was placed on a wooden bench, and Mary Woodhouse got busy ladling out a delicious-smelling chicken soup into six fat mugs.

The Quaker woman handed a mug of soup and a slice of bread to each person, stopping to admire baby Toby who was contentedly sucking his fingers. When she came to Rosebud, who was trying to keep from coughing long enough to sip the hot soup, the woman looked at her closely and put her hand on the girl's forehead.

"This child is not well!" she said, looking up at the others with alarm. "Her clothes are damp and she's shivering. We must get her to bed right away, or we will have a case of pneumonia on our hands!"

Chapter 10

Slave Catcher!

MARY WOODHOUSE WANTED to take Rosebud to the house immediately, but her husband insisted that they wait until dark. "We must be very careful," he said. "Go ahead, Isaac, tell your mother and Mrs. Tubman what you told me."

Rosebud, who was trying to swallow the hot soup in spite of her sore throat, jumped at the sound of the boy's name. She didn't like this white boy having the same name as her brother. Every time someone said "Isaac," she expected her brother to suddenly appear.

"Well, Ma'am," the boy was saying to Harriet, "I took one of Papa's horses into Petersburg to the blacksmith this morning—"

"Petersburg!" exclaimed Harriet Tubman. "Have

we crossed the state line into Delaware?"

"Yes, Ma'am. Anyway, there was a stranger there having his horse shod. I heard him tell the blacksmith that he was looking for some slaves who'd run away from the Tidewater Flats down near Bucktown in Maryland . . ."

Sally gave a frightened cry and pulled the baby closer.

" . . . but they'd given him the slip in the swamp ten miles downriver," Isaac went on. "And then it rained very hard, he said, which made tracking with dogs nearly impossible. But he was sure the runaways were following the river and coming this way. He said there was a big reward . . ."

At the mention of a reward, the runaways shifted uneasily. "I knew all this sweetness and light had a stinkin' center," Charles muttered under his breath, and began edging slowly toward the door. But Benjamin Woodhouse's eye caught his movement.

"No, no, Mr. Walker," he said. "I assure thee, young Isaac is only telling what the stranger *said*. A Quaker would never betray a fellow human being for a reward, or we would be as guilty as Judas Iscariot who betrayed our Lord in Gethsemane for thirty pieces of silver!"

Isaac looked bewildered by the effect of his words on the anxious runaways. He looked at his father. "Go on, Isaac," Benjamin encouraged him.

"Well, I—I was afraid that the runaway slaves were going to be caught unless someone helped them. Friend Thomas had told Papa that runaways often hide in the woods during the day, so I decided to go looking for thee."

"Glory to God that you found us instead of the slave catchers!" said Harriet.

"But . . . if the dogs pick up our trail, that trail is going to lead right here," said Tobias soberly.

The room was silent except for Rosebud's coughing as everyone realized the truth of what he'd said.

Then Benjamin Woodhouse spoke. "Maybe, maybe not. I have an idea. . . ."

Rosebud snuggled under the duck-down comforter in the little attic room. She had never been in such a soft, warm bed! It would be so pleasant . . . if only she didn't feel so sick.

They had waited in the Quaker meetinghouse until dark, and then Mr. Woodhouse had told them to walk back down the road, the way they had come. Rosebud had stumbled along, leaning on Mary, wondering what was happening and wishing she could go to sleep, when along came a wagon behind them with Mr. Woodhouse driving a team of horses! The Quaker man picked them up, and by taking the long way around, drove the wagon back to the Woodhouse farm. Mary whispered in her ear that he was doing it to fool the slave catcher's dogs.

At the house, Mary and Mrs. Woodhouse had stripped off Rosebud's damp underclothes, pulled one of Mrs. Woodhouse's flannel night dresses over her head, and tucked her in this bed. It had taken a long time to stop shivering, but now she was warm and drowsy.

Rosebud slept fitfully the rest of that night and all the next day, waking from time to time with a terrible coughing fit that seemed like it was going to rip out her insides.

As the room began to get dark again, Harriet Tubman came into the little attic room and sat on the bed.

"Rosebud? Are you awake?"

The girl nodded miserably.

"There's something I want to tell you. When I first ran away to freedom, the way sometimes got hard. But deep down in my soul, I knew there was one of two things I had a right to: liberty or death. If I could not have one, I would have the other. I was determined that no slave catcher should take me alive; I would fight for my liberty as long as my strength lasted, and when the time came for me to go, the Lord would let them take me."

Just then Rosebud had a coughing fit and Harriet helped her with a drink of water. Then Rosebud sank back onto the soft pillow. Why was Harriet telling her this? The Woodhouses seemed like nice white

104

folks; they were safe now, weren't they? Besides, Rosebud always felt safe with Harriet. She always seemed to know what to do.

"Now you listen to me," Harriet said, gripping the girl's shoulders. "When things get tough, I want you to say this prayer: 'Lord, I'm goin' to hold steady on to You, and You've got to see me through.' Can you say that?"

Rosebud nodded. "Lord, I'm a-goin' to hold steady on to You, and You've got to see me through," she repeated hoarsely.

"Good girl. Now, you sleep. You need to get better."

It wasn't until the next morning that Rosebud learned that Harriet Tubman and the rest of her fellow runaways had headed north once more under cover of darkness and left her behind.

Rosebud pulled away from Mary Woodhouse's hand and turned her face to the wall, sobbing into the pillow.

"Don't cry so, child," said the motherly woman. "Thou art too sick to continue the journey. They had no choice but to go without thee."

"Th—th—they could've waited t—t—till I'm better," Rosebud hiccuped in a muffled voice.

"Humph. It's much harder hiding seven black souls than one, in a small white family. Nay, I agree with Mrs. Tubman; they needed to push on to the next station. They will wait for thee in Philadel-phia."

Philadelphia! That was another fifty miles—Mary had told her that much. She was only halfway to freedom. But she could never make it alone. She didn't know the way! An overwhelming feeling of despair set off new sobs into the pillow.

Later that afternoon, it was Isaac who came up to the little attic room with some hot broth for their patient. "What day is it?" Rosebud asked hoarsely.

"Why, it's Sixth Day," said Isaac.

Sixth day? What a funny way of talking these Quakers had! But Rosebud was too proud to ask what he meant. She thought a moment; if Sunday was the first day of the week, then sixth day would be Friday. "Issue Day" at the Powers Plantation had been the first Saturday of October, and she had run away that night . . . which meant she'd been gone six days already. Only six days? It felt like a lifetime!

She realized Isaac was staring at her. "Thee has been crying," he said finally.

Rosebud looked away.

"Don't worry," Isaac said. "My mother will take good care of thee. And thee can use my room as long as thee likes."

Startled, Rosebud turned her head back and stared at the boy. *His room?* It had never occurred to her that he had given up his room for her. She just thought all white people had extra rooms in their houses.

That day and all the next, Rosebud worried. The

Woodhouses were being very nice to her, true, but she didn't want to stay here any longer. She wanted to be with Harriet Tubman and the others. She wanted to find her pappy. But how? She felt so alone—more alone than she'd felt since her mammy died and her pappy had run away.

By the next day, Rosebud was feeling much better, even though she was still coughing. "That's good, that's good," Mrs. Woodhouse said. "Thee has to get all that stuff out of thy chest. Now here . . . put these on and come down to supper tonight. Thee must get thy strength back." And she laid Rosebud's dresses, bandana, and shawl on the bed, freshly washed and dried.

At suppertime, Rosebud got dressed and timidly made her way down the narrow stairs. Mary Woodhouse was setting supper on a plain wooden table, nicely crafted, with four straight-backed chairs around it. Benjamin Woodhouse smiled at Rosebud and held a chair for her. Then the rest of the family sat and bowed their heads while Benjamin said a blessing.

As the food was served, Mary chatted away, asking Rosebud questions about her family, but Rosebud was so nervous sitting at the same table with a white family that she could only nod yes or no. Finally Benjamin saw her distress and guided the conversation away from the girl.

"Tomorrow is First Day, Papa," said Isaac. "Can Rosebud come with us to Worship Meeting?"

Rosebud looked startled. She'd never been to

church before. But a *white* church?

"No, I'm afraid not," said Benjamin, shaking his head.

"But, Papa!" Isaac protested.

Rosebud didn't know whether to be disappointed or relieved. But it was just as she thought. White folks—even Quakers—didn't want black folks in their church.

"Don't forget that Rosebud, young as she is, is a runaway," Benjamin explained. "We are *hiding* her. No one must know she is here."

"Well, then, in that case, I will stay home to keep her company," said Isaac.

Again his father shook his head. "Then people will wonder where thou art, and we don't want to tell a lie. We must do everything just as we always do. We will go to Meeting tomorrow, and Rosebud must stay here."

The next morning the Woodhouse family walked through the woods to the Quaker meetinghouse, leaving Rosebud at home. As the hours ticked away on the wall clock in the front hall, Rosebud thought, *This is my chance. I could leave now, and no one would stop me.* But then she realized she did not know how to find her friends. She could go back and follow the Choptank River, but Harriet had said that it soon dwindled to a creek in Delaware. Where would she go then? And she didn't have a travel pass. Any white person could stop any black person at any time and demand to see a pass from his or her master; it was the law.

With a sinking feeling, Rosebud realized she was trapped, just as much as if she were tied up in the stable, as her brother Isaac had been.

The next morning, Rosebud got dressed and came down to the kitchen where Mrs. Woodhouse was bustling about.

"Mrs. Woodhouse . . . Ma'am," Rosebud ventured. "When will I be able to leave and join my friends in Philadelphia?"

"Soon, dear, soon," said Mrs. Woodhouse, fanning the wood in the cast iron stove and tucking a stray wisp of brown hair under her starched white cap. "We must be sure that thou art completely well . . . oh, here." She handed Rosebud a basket. "Will thee go out to the barn and gather some eggs for our breakfast? I cannot make this fire burn right!"

With a sigh, Rosebud took the basket and let herself out the back door of the house. As she rounded the corner and started down the path to the barn, she was startled to see Isaac talking to a strange man in the barnyard. She stopped and stood uncertainly, not sure what to do. Then her mouth went completely dry.

The man talking to Isaac Woodhouse was the white-haired slave catcher that had taken her brother away on the chain gang!

At just that moment, Isaac looked up and saw her. In a flash his face contorted into an angry scowl. "You lazy, good-for-nothing girl!" he shouted. "Get that broom and sweep the path like Mama told thee to!"

Rosebud was shocked. She started to protest, to tell Isaac that his mama wanted her to gather eggs, but he came toward her with his hand raised as if to strike her. She looked around frantically and saw an old broom leaning against the house. Dropping the basket, she started sweeping the path furiously, sending bits of dried leaves and grass flying.

Isaac went back to talking to the slave catcher. Rosebud's heart was beating wildly. Would the man remember her? He didn't seem to; maybe because she was wearing a bandana and a woman's dress now, instead of the tow-linen shirt she'd worn as a child last spring. But what could explain Isaac's sudden change in behavior? Unless . . . unless she'd been tricked. The Woodhouses had let the other runaways go, but maybe they had kept her behind to make her their slave!

After a few minutes Isaac yelled at her again. "All right, that's enough. Now pick up that basket and get those eggs. Hurry! Don't keep Mama waiting all day!"

Bewildered, Rosebud picked up the basket she'd dropped and ran to the barn, ducking inside its huge doors into the cool, dark interior. She could hear the man laughing behind her. The sweeping and running made her start to cough again, causing tears to well up in her eyes. What was happening? Why was Isaac talking to that evil man?

She peeked out the door into the barnyard. She could see some big papers rolled up under the man's arm. As she watched, he took one out and unrolled it

for Isaac to see. Rosebud squinted hard and then gasped. It was a drawing of Harriet Tubman, she was sure of it!

Just then Isaac looked up and yelled, "What are thee lookin' at, girl? Get back in there and fetch those eggs!"

As Rosebud turned away, she heard the man continue, "There's a big fat reward for anyone who catches this she-devil," he said, grinning. "*And* for the niggers she's got with her. Slave owners are tired of their slaves disappearing when she comes around."

"I don't blame them." Isaac nodded. "That's some reward—twenty thousand dollars!"

"Yep. Well, you take this here poster and put it on

your fence, like you said. Somebody somewhere is gonna git her. Maybe it'll be you!" And he laughed again. "Meantime, you're doin' a pretty good job keepin' Sassy there in line—heh, heh."

Rosebud saw Isaac take the poster and wave as the man mounted his horse and start back down the road.

With a sinking heart, Rosebud shrank back against the inside of the barn door. Now she knew the truth. It was a trap. Either they would let her go, and follow her, so that she would lead them to Harriet Tubman . . . or they would keep her here, hoping Harriet would come back for her.

Either way, freedom seemed to be slipping from her grasp.

Chapter 11

I Am Rosalie! I Am Free!

ROSEBUD REALIZED that Isaac Woodhouse was heading for the barn. She quickly scurried toward the sound of cackling chickens and discovered a row of neat wooden boxes along the back wall.

"Scat!" she hissed to a fat hen on one of the nests. The hen protested loudly. Thrusting her shaking hand into the straw, Rosebud pulled out a smooth, warm egg.

"Rosebud?"

Isaac's voice startled her. She slowly put the egg in her basket but did not turn around.

"Rosebud, I'm sorry for how I spoke to thee out there! But that was a slave catcher! He was looking for Harriet Tubman and the rest of you. When thee came out of the house, I had to make him think that thee . . . uh, that thee . . . well, I didn't want him to get suspicious!"

Rosebud was silent.

Isaac's voice sounded miserable. "Rosebud, thou must believe me! I did it to fool him. But . . . but I know it hurt thee badly."

Rosebud squeezed her eyes shut and two tears ran down her cheeks. She felt so confused. One minute this white boy was yelling at her and treating her just like a slave; the next he was apologizing and talking to her in a kind way. *Oh, Lord,* she cried inside, *I'm tryin' to hold steady on to You . . . but I'm all mixed up and don't know what to do!*

Ignoring Isaac, Rosebud finished gathering nine brown eggs and walked back to the house, fighting back the tears. Without a word she set the egg basket on the kitchen table and walked up the narrow stairs to the attic room. Below her she could hear Mrs. Woodhouse's anxious voice. "Rosebud? Is something wrong? . . . Isaac! What happened?"

Alone at last, Rosebud let the tears come, wave after wave of fear and loneliness and confusion. Exhausted from crying, Rosebud finally slept.

When she awoke in late afternoon, her stomach hurt with hunger. She hadn't had anything to eat all day. But as she crept down the attic stairs, she heard voices arguing in the dining room.

The stairs creaked and the voices stopped. Mrs. Woodhouse came to the open doorway. "Why, hello, Rosebud. Did you have a good sleep? You must be hungry, poor child!" The Quaker woman steered the girl into the kitchen and within minutes set a plate in front of her with two lovely fried eggs, two large muffins, a slice of fried ham, and a mug of cool milk.

Rosebud's mouth watered. As she ate, Benjamin Woodhouse also came into the kitchen, followed by Isaac. "Isaac told us about the slave catcher that came to the farm today," he said. "I am proud that he acted so quickly to keep that evil man from suspecting that thou art a runaway. But we know it was very upsetting. We are all sorry. Thee must forgive him."

Rosebud stared at her plate. Forgive Isaac? Did that mean telling him it was all right to call her "lazy" and "good-for-nothing"? She couldn't!

Mr. Woodhouse cleared his throat. "This incident has forced us to come to a decision. Thee must leave, Rosebud. It is no longer safe here. If the slave catcher asked around, our neighbors would tell him that we have no slaves."

His wife started to protest, but Mr. Woodhouse held up his hand. "Mrs. Woodhouse thinks thou art not yet well enough, but we must take that chance. Thee must leave tonight. Now . . . we must get ready."

Rosebud tried not to show her dismay. Tonight? Were they just turning her loose? But she didn't know where to go! If the slave catcher found her alone on the road or in the woods, he would surely know she was a runaway! But she obediently went upstairs and rolled her extra dress and blanket into a bundle. She retied her mammy's bandana neatly

115

around her head, put on her shawl, and waited for it to get dark.

Finally she heard Mrs. Woodhouse call her.

"Oh, Lord, I'm tryin' to hold steady on to You . . ." she breathed as she walked down the narrow stairs for the last time.

Mrs. Woodhouse handed her a bundle of food and gave her a motherly hug. "Go quickly, child. They're waiting for you in the barn."

Rosebud walked uncertainly to the barn. Who was waiting—Mr. Woodhouse? Was he going to tell her where to go? There was no light inside, but as she pulled the door open, she heard Mr. Woodhouse's voice. "Ah, there you are, young lady. Now up you go." The next thing she knew, he was helping her climb into the seat of the farm wagon. And from the wagon seat, Isaac held out a hand and pulled her up beside him.

"Isaac is going to drive thee to find thy friends— all the way to Philadelphia, if need be," said Mr. Woodhouse. "Now, go and Godspeed."

Rosebud rode silently beside Isaac as the team of horses headed north. She felt ashamed. The Woodhouses had been very kind to her since Isaac had found them out in the woods. And Isaac's upsetting behavior that morning had kept the slave catcher from knowing she was a runaway. And yet . . . doubts still nagged at her. What about all that reward money? Could Isaac be using her to get to Harriet Tubman?

It was so hard to know whom to trust! No white person had ever been her friend in all her thirteen years. And yet, if she was wrong about Isaac, she was being very ungrateful.

"Art thou cold?" Isaac asked, finally breaking the silence.

"No. My shawl is warm."

They rode on in silence once more. It was Isaac who again spoke first. "Is Rosebud thy real name?"

She hesitated. Many slaves were given nicknames by their masters, who might not bother to know a slave's full name. But Rosebud was the only name she had ever known. "My mammy said I was born when the rosebuds came out."

"What about the rest of your family? Do they have unusual names like you?"

Before Rosebud realized what was happening, she was telling Isaac about Abe and Sarah Jackson, and her brother Isaac, and about Isaac running away and getting caught and being dragged away on the chain gang. As she talked, all the loneliness of the last days and weeks and months seemed to come spilling out in words.

She told about burying baby Matthew and her mammy, and how one night her pappy had heard someone singing, "Go down, Moses," outside the cabin, and that was the last time she saw him. But he had told her to "listen for the whippoorwill" after harvest . . . and that's how she ended up with Harriet

Tubman and the others, running north to freedom. "But most of all," Rosebud said, "I just want to find my pappy again."

Isaac was thoughtful for several minutes. "Abe . . . Sarah . . . Isaac. Did you know thy family is named after one of the most famous families in the Bible?"

Rosebud shook her head.

"Abraham loved God, and God promised that he would be the father of a great nation. The only problem was, Abraham and Sarah were very old and didn't have any children. It looked impossible! But they believed God's promise, and sure enough, they finally had a baby and named him Isaac."

Isaac laughed. "That's why my parents named me Isaac," he confided. "They waited a long time for me, too. Anyway," he went on, "after many years, Abraham's family became so big, no one could even count them. They became God's chosen people, the Jews—the same people Moses led out of slavery."

Rosebud was astonished. Why hadn't she ever heard this story before? Think of it! Her pappy and mammy and her brother were named after a famous family in the Bible.

They had been traveling along the road for hours and the sky was starting to get light. Rosebud thought about what Isaac had said.

"Do you think that promise could be true for my family?" she ventured. "About becoming a family—again—even though it looks impossible?"

"Sure. Why not? In the Bible God was always doing impossible things."

"Even finding my brother Isaac?"

Isaac Woodhouse grinned. "Especially thy brother Isaac. After all, he is Abraham and Sarah's son, right?"

Isaac pulled off the road at daybreak to give the horses a rest and let them munch on the grass. After eating some of the food that Mary Woodhouse had packed, Rosebud fell asleep under a tree. But a few hours later they were on their way again.

"When we go through a town, thee must sit in the back of the wagon," Isaac said. "I am sorry. But Delaware is still a slave state; we must not make anyone suspicious."

Rosebud meekly submitted to this indignity. She realized that Isaac was doing it for her good.

They rested the horses again in late afternoon, then started again at twilight. "We are coming near to Wilmington," Isaac told Rosebud. "That is where Friend Thomas Garrett lives. That was where Mrs. Tubman was heading—he will know what has happened to thy friends."

But as they drew near the city, they saw first one, then another, then *another* poster with the picture of Harriet Tubman on it.

"We may have trouble here," Isaac murmured. "Wilmington is so close to the state line that the slave catchers and bounty hunters will be on the alert, trying to stop any runaways from getting into

Pennsylvania."

Rosebud was scared. She was so close to freedom! What if she got caught now?

Isaac had an idea. "Rosebud, wrap thy blanket around thee and lie under the wagon seat. Try not to move—and don't cough! It's dark enough, no one will see thee." Rosebud did as she was told, and at the last minute Isaac took off his flat-brimmed Quaker hat and stuffed it under the wagon seat as well.

Inside the blanket under the wagon seat, Rose-

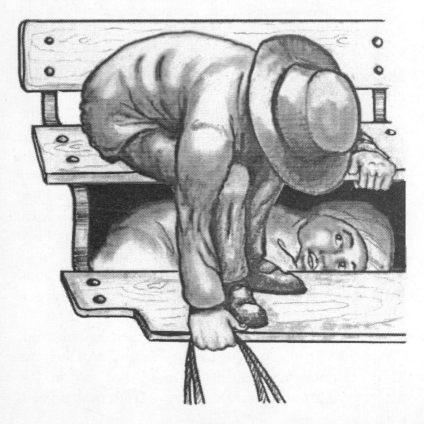

bud could feel every rock and rut in the road. Gradually there were more noises, too—horses and carts rumbling along the road, people hailing each other, laughter from the inns along the road.

"Be very quiet," Isaac murmured. "We are coming to a bridge and there are people about."

"Hey, you, boy! Stop!" said a gruff voice.

Under the blanket, Rosebud held her breath.

"Have you seen any runaway slaves?" said the voice. It came from someone standing right beside the wagon wheel. "We're lookin' for a certain group o' darkies—tall, skinny man . . . young wench with a baby . . . 'nother young man . . . young girl 'bout ten or twelve . . ."

"Don't fergit the fox!" yelled another voice, laughing.

"You mean this one?" said Isaac. Rosebud heard the rustle of paper. Then she realized he had said "you" instead of "thee."

"I see you got one o' them posters," chuckled the first voice.

"Yep," said Isaac. "With the kind of money be-

$20,000
REWARD

Harriet Tubman
Alias "Moses" – Has scar on forehead
Cannot read or write – Contact
Dr. Anthony Thompson
Bucktown, Maryland

ing offered for that Tubman woman, I plan to start hunting as soon as I get home—right after supper."

"Well, get along with you, then. But don't be pickin' up no strangers."

The wagon lurched forward and made a terrible racket as the horses clomped over the wooden bridge that led into Wilmington, Delaware. It seemed a long time before Isaac finally said, "Whoa!" and then, "Thee can come out now. We are here."

Rosebud crawled stiffly out from under the wagon seat. The wagon was pulled into a narrow alley beside what looked like a shoe shop. Isaac helped her down, and they knocked softly on a door in the back.

"Who's there?"

"Uh . . . I have a small package for thee," said Isaac. He'd obviously been instructed by Harriet Tubman in "underground railroad" language.

The door was unlatched and the two young people were quickly pulled in. Rosebud saw an elderly white gentleman with a round clean-shaven face and plump jowls. "Harriet! Harriet Tubman!" he called happily. "Your package has arrived."

Rosebud was amazed to discover that Harriet and the others had only arrived at Thomas Garrett's "station" the night before. She and Isaac had covered as many miles by wagon in twenty-four hours as the others had in five nights of walking. "Don't worry none, child," Mary assured her. "Ain't no way all of us could've come by wagon without getting stopped by slave catchers."

The next morning Isaac prepared to head home. But first he took Rosebud aside. "I've been thinking," he said. "Thy brother has the same name as I do. That makes us spiritual kinsfolk in a way . . . and, well, I've been thinking about the promise God made to Abraham. And I want to make a promise to thee."

A promise? What was Isaac talking about?

Isaac took a big breath. "I'm fifteen now; soon I'll be a man. But as soon as father can spare me from the farm, I am going to find thy brother, and I will help him run away—or . . . or I will buy him and set him free! That is my promise. But . . . thee must realize, it might take a long time."

Rosebud was speechless. No one had ever made her a promise before. But she believed Isaac. Someday . . . someday, he would help her brother be free.

"Thank you, Isaac," she whispered. Tears blurred her eyes.

"Oh! And something else!" Isaac looked a little embarrassed. "May I call thee Rosalie? Rosebud is nice—but it seems to me the rosebud has grown up and become a flower. In fact," Isaac twisted his hat in his hands, "you are the bravest girl I have ever met."

Again Rosebud didn't know what to say. She tried the word in her mind: *Rosalie.* It had a nice sound—a new sound.

Isaac seemed to read her mind. "You used to be Rosebud, the slave. But now you could be Rosalie, the free woman."

Rosebud nodded. She tried it out. "I am Rosalie. I am free."

Then she laughed aloud. What a wonderful sound! *I am Rosalie! I am free!*

Chapter 12

The Freedom Train

WHERE ARE THY SHOES, young lady?" questioned Thomas Garrett gravely when Rosalie joined the others for breakfast in a small secret room at the back of Garrett's shoe shop.

Rosalie looked down at her bare feet and shook her head. "I got my first pair on Issue Day—the day I ran away—but they pinched my toes and I didn't think I could run very far."

Garrett chuckled. "Well, let's see what we can do for thee. Stockings would help."

Sure enough, after breakfast the old gentleman brought a pair of stockings and a pair of shoes for Rosalie to try on. They felt funny, but the leather was soft and the shoes laced firmly up to her ankles.

"Wear them around the house—thee will get used

to them. And thee will need shoes up north in the winter!" said Mr. Garrett.

The kindly gentleman also gave new shoes from his shop to the other runaways, whose old shoes were falling apart from the long trek through the woods and water.

Rosalie was glad to be back with Harriet and the others—even the sour-faced Charles Walker. They hid all day in Garrett's secret room, and that evening he came and outlined the plan for the next day.

"Philadelphia is only twenty miles across the border, but it is probably the most dangerous part of thy trip," he told them. "I have arranged for a bricklayer who is sympathetic to our cause to drive thee into Philadelphia—but thee must go in daytime, just like any other load of bricks."

Even Harriet looked puzzled.

"The bricklayer has built a false floor in the bottom of the wagon; that is where thee will lie. Then the wagon will be loaded with bricks. No slave-catcher wants to unload a wagonful of bricks! It is a trick we have used before, and it has worked well . . . although not very comfortable for the passengers, I admit. As for the baby . . . Harriet, does thee have thy—?"

Harriet held up the brown bottle from her pocket.

"Good," said Garrett. "Thee will need to keep the baby quiet until thee gets to Philadelphia. There William Still, a free black man with the Vigilance Committee, is expecting thee."

"Will we be free then?" asked Rosalie eagerly.

"Yes . . . and no. Pennsylvania is a free state. But under the accursed Fugitive Slave Law"—Garrett's forehead knitted angrily—"a slave catcher can follow a runaway slave into a free state and still drag him back to his former master. I urge thee all to keep going!"

"But where?" several voices chorused.

"To Canada."

Rosalie would never forget the ride from Wilmington to Philadelphia under the load of bricks. Before sunup the next morning, they all lay down

head to toe in the bottom of the bricklayer's wagon, and a false floor was laid over them. Rosalie could hear the thump, thump, thump as the heavy bricks were stacked on top.

She wanted to scream. It felt like being buried alive! But Harriet patted her comfortingly. "Shh, shh. It'll be all right, child. Say the prayer."

Oh, Lord, I'm goin' to hold steady on to You, and You've got to see me through . . .

The wagon rattled and shook mile after mile. Every now and then they heard the driver say, "Whoa!" and voices would demand to know what kind of load he carried. But one look at the bricks and they were always waved on.

Late that afternoon the wagon was unloaded in the heart of the city of Philadelphia, behind a brick building that housed the Vigilance Committee—a group of black and white abolitionists whose sole purpose was to help runaway slaves. William Still, the secretary, ushered the weary group into the committee's office and took down all their names in a record book. He was the first black man Rosalie had ever seen wearing a suit, starched white shirt, and tie.

"Rosalie Jackson," Rosalie said when it was her turn to give her name.

Harriet and the others looked at her in surprise.

"My name is Rosalie. I am free!" the girl said firmly.

At that everyone broke into grins and cheers.

"You got that right, young lady," said Mr. Still.

"Now we are going to try to keep you that way."

To Rosalie's amazement, they were given train tickets and transported the next day in two buggies to the Philadelphia train station. There they climbed into a real passenger coach and sat in real seats at the back of the train car with several other black folks. As Mr. Still handed Harriet a large hamper of food, he said, "You better lie low for a while, Harriet. They've got a price on your head now."

The small woman nodded. "I know. But it ain't ever stopped me before, and it ain't goin' to stop me now. I still got family back in the Tidewater Flats—especially my pappy Ben and my mammy Old 'Rit. I want them to die free."

Mr. Still shrugged, as if he knew it was useless to argue, and got off the train just as the whistle blew.

Rosalie couldn't get over riding in an actual train behind a real steam engine. "Is this the *real* underground railroad?" she asked Harriet curiously.

"No, Rosalie," Harriet smiled. "If you have money for a ticket, anyone can ride this train."

As the miles clicked away outside the train windows, Rosalie realized she was going farther and farther from home. She heard the conductor call out the names of the stations: Allentown . . . Scranton . . . Binghamton.

"We're in New York State now," Harriet told her.

Rosalie held baby Toby up to the window, pointing out the cows and horses grazing in the bright October sunlight. As she watched whole forests of trees march past—all gold and red and yellow and green—a tight lump formed in her throat. How would she ever find her pappy now? She was going so far away! And how would her brother ever find her, if Isaac Woodhouse kept his promise? She wanted to be free; she didn't ever want to be a slave again! But . . . would she ever see her family?

The steam engine pulling their train chugged through the countryside all that day and all through the night. The hard benches were uncomfortable, but snuggled against Mary's shoulder, Rosalie somehow fell asleep, jolted awake from time to time when the train pulled into yet another station.

"Rosalie. Rosalie, wake up." Mary was shaking her. "If you're gonna have a big name like Rosalie," her friend complained good-naturedly, pushing Rosalie's head off her lap, "you're gonna have to sleep on your own. My leg is asleep!"

Rosalie stretched. Sunlight was pouring into the train windows, and passengers were getting their bags together.

"We're coming into Niagara," Harriet informed them. "This is where we get off."

When the weary travelers got off the train, Rosalie could hear an immense roar. She wanted to ask what it was, but Harriet was already heading out of the train station and down the street. The others hustled to keep up. Between the neat wooden buildings lining the street—a ladies dress shop, hotel, saddle shop, and blacksmith—Rosalie caught glimpses of a big gorge with trees on the other side, and the roar was getting louder.

Harriet turned at a break in the buildings and walked toward the sound. As they turned another corner, Rosalie saw a sight she had never dreamed of in her whole life.

In front of them stood a deep gorge. To their left, a river poured over a wide, steep cliff into the gorge in a massive waterfall, thundering loudly and sending a cloud of white spray into the air. But beyond the first waterfall, another arm of the river was pouring into the gorge, three times larger and shaped like a big horseshoe. The roar was deafening.

"Niagara Falls!" Harriet shouted over the thundering sound. "That's Ontario, Canada, on the other side. And freedom!"

The little group stood in speechless wonder for several minutes before Harriet hurried them on. They followed the road along the gorge away from the falls, walking about two miles north, until they came to a bridge over the river. "The Niagara River flows north from Lake Erie into Lake Ontario and finally into the ocean," Harriet explained as the little group stood staring at the narrow suspension bridge hanging over the deepest part of the gorge. The water was far below.

Since the bridge was only one lane wide, the little group had to wait their turn while a farmer's wagon rumbled across from the other side. In spite of herself, Rosebud's knees shook at the thought of walking over the deep chasm on that wobbly bridge.

"William Still gave us papers to help us get into Canada," Harriet assured the others as they waited. They were standing off to the side, hoping to not attract attention.

Rosalie didn't say much. Freedom—real freedom—lay just across the river on the other side. The slave catchers couldn't take a runaway slave back from Canada. William Still had told them that Canada didn't have to obey the Fugitive Slave Law.

Finally it was their turn to cross the bridge. Harriet gave them each a coin, donated by the Vigilance Committee back in Philadelphia, to pay the bridge toll. Dutifully, Rosalie paid her toll and stepped onto the bridge. She did not dare look down. But halfway across, Rosalie stopped and stared back at the United States—the country where she had been born and raised a slave. *Goodbye. Goodbye to slavery!* But at the same time Rosalie felt sad. Somehow the thought of freedom didn't feel so wonderful without her family.

As they stepped off the bridge on the other side, Rosalie held back a little behind Harriet, Charles,

Mary, Tobias and Sally, and little Toby. Their journey was over. But what would they do now?

Rosalie waited numbly while a customs agent checked their papers that Harriet handed him. Then suddenly she heard her name.

"Rosebud! Rosebud Jackson!"

Her head jerked up. Who was calling her name?

She saw a black man running toward her, dodging people who were milling about with bags and boxes. The man looked familiar, big and square and handsome—

"Pappy!" she screamed. And the next moment she was being caught up into Abe Jackson's strong arms and kissed all over her face.

Rosalie could hardly breathe for happiness. Over Pappy's shoulder she saw Harriet Tubman laughing. Harriet had known all the time, known that she was bringing her home—home to her pappy!

"Oh, Baby," Abe murmured as he finally set her down. "I've been watching the bridge for days, knowin' you were comin'. Miz Tubman said she would bring you . . . and she did, she did." And he caught her up again in a big bear hug.

"Pappy," Rosalie whispered in his ear. "I've got something to tell you. My name isn't Rosebud anymore. *I am Rosalie. And I am free!*"

More About Harriet Tubman

A ROUND 1820, A SLAVE BABY was born to Ben and Harriet ("Old 'Rit") Ross in the slave quarter of a tobacco plantation situated in the Tidewater Flats of Maryland, along the Eastern Shore of Chesapeake Bay. The little girl was named Araminta ("Minty" for short) and, like the rest of her brothers and sisters, was enthralled by the Bible stories, songs, and spirituals taught by their deeply religious mother.

Edward Brodas, the plantation owner, was not a cruel master, but times were hard and sometimes he had to "hire out" his slaves to make ends meet. When Minty was six years old, she was hired out to Mrs. Cook, a weaver, who needed a girl to help her wind yarn. But Minty was stubborn and did not want to learn to weave. In frustration, Mrs. Cook sent her off with Mr. Cook to help him set muskrat traps, which Minty liked better. But the constant damp and cold brought on a severe case of measles, after which Minty always had a husky voice.

At age seven, Minty was again hired out to a "Miss Susan" to help care for her baby. Minty's job was to keep the baby from crying and waking Miss Susan at night—leaving the young girl exhausted. After Miss Susan beat her for taking some sugar, Minty ran away and spent five days hiding in a pigpen.

By now the Brodas Plantation was in serious financial trouble. Edward Brodas did not like separating families, but two of Minty's older sisters had been sold "down South" to one of the slave traders who came through Maryland regularly. Being sold "down South" struck terror in the hearts of the slaves and was used as a threat to keep them from running away. It meant never seeing family and home again, with the probability of being sold to a cruel master.

Fear was stalking the land. Denmark Vesey, a free Negro, and one-hundred-thirty slaves were executed for plotting a violent slave insurrection. After that, slaves were not permitted to be out at night or gather in groups (even for worship) or sing the comforting Negro spirituals, such as "Go down, Moses . . . Tell old Pharaoh, Let my people go!"

In the meantime, realizing young Minty was hopeless at domestic work, Brodas hired her out as a field hand. It was hard work, but Minty liked being outdoors, and by age eleven she had a strong, erect body and calloused hands. She had taken to wearing a woman's bandana around her head and had shed the pet name of Minty. Folks called her Harriet, now, after her mother.

When Harriet was thirteen, one of the field slaves tried to run away during cornhusking time. In an effort to stop him, the overseer threw a two-pound weight at him, but Harriet stood in his way and the missile hit the young girl in the forehead instead. She was unconscious for days, then slipped in and out of a stupor for months. As Harriet slowly recovered, a constant prayer was on her lips—for her master: "Change his heart, Lord, convert him."

Even though Harriet recovered, she suffered severe headaches and peculiar sleeping fits for the rest of her life. As winter turned to spring, the rumor being whispered in the slave quarter was that Harriet and her brothers would be sold to the next slave trader. Rebellion surged in her heart, and her prayer changed. "Lord, if you're never going to change Massa Brodas' heart—then kill him Lord! Take him out of the way."

Within weeks Edward Brodas became ill . . . and died even before the new tobacco crop had been planted. Conscience-stricken, Harriet thought she had killed him! "Oh, Lord," she cried out, "I would give the world full of silver and gold to bring that poor soul back. . . . I would give myself. I would give everything!"

Edward Brodas had promised Ben and Old 'Rit

that they would have their freedom when he died. But all his will stated was that none of his slaves could be sold outside the state of Maryland. Brodas' heir was very young, so his guardian, a Dr. Anthony Thompson from nearby Bucktown, administered the plantation.

Soon Ben Ross and his daughter were hired out to a Mr. Stewart, a builder. Harriet asked Mr. Stewart if she could work in the woods with her father instead of being a housekeeper, and was granted permission. Soon she was swinging a broadaxe, cutting timber, hauling logs, plowing fields, and driving an oxcart. At the same time she was learning woodlore from her father: how to tell direction by the moss growing on the north side of the trees and the north star at night; how to walk quietly through the woods like the Indians so as not to disturb the woodland creatures, and how to make bird calls.

In 1844, at the age of twenty-four, Harriet married a free Negro named John Tubman, bringing a handmade patchwork quilt as part of her trousseau. But she was still a slave, working as a field hand for Doc Thompson. She talked to her husband about running away, but he said it was foolishness; in fact, he would tell her master if she tried it! That hurt her deeply. After that, she stopped talking about running away but she thought about it all the time.

In 1849, the young Brodas heir died, and Doc Thompson began making plans to sell slaves "down South." This time Harriet's mind was made up: "There was one of two things I had a right to, liberty or death. If I could not have one, I would have the other, for no man should take me alive. I would fight for my liberty as long as my strength lasted, and when the time came for me to go, the Lord would let them take me."

Now Harriet's daily prayer became, "Lord, I'm going to hold steady on to You, and You've got to see me through." She had heard about an "underground railroad" that took slaves to freedom in the northern states. One night she took her patchwork quilt and silently made her way through the woods to Bucktown. She knew a white Quaker lady there who had once said, "If you ever need help, come to me." There she learned that the Underground Railroad was not a railroad at all, but a network of "stations" (sympathetic farmers and townspeople) who would hide slaves and help them reach freedom.

Leaving her quilt with the Quaker lady as a gift, Harriet set off on her long journey on foot. She traveled only at night, using all the woodlore she knew to make her way north. At each friendly "station," she was told where to go next. Along the way she traveled in a wagon under a load of vegetables, was rowed up the Choptank River by a man she had never seen before, was concealed in a haystack, spent a week hidden in a potato hole in a cabin that belonged to a family of free Negroes, was hidden in the attic of a Quaker family, and was befriended by stout German farmers. Still afflicted with her head injury, she sometimes fell asleep right on the road, but somehow managed to escape detection.

Approaching Wilmington, Delaware, Harriet had been instructed to hide in a graveyard. A man came wandering through muttering, "I have a ticket for the railroad." This man disguised Harriet in workmen's clothes and took her to Thomas Garrett's house, a famous Quaker abolitionist. Garrett, who had a shoe shop, gave her new shoes and fancy women's clothes and drove her in his buggy north of Wilmington. Before she went on he gave Harriet, who couldn't read or write, a paper with the word *PENNSYLVANIA* written on it so she could recognize when she crossed the state line.

When Harriet finally crossed into Pennsylvania, she had traveled ninety miles. "I looked at my hands to see if I was the same person, now I was free," she said later. "There was such a glory over everything. The sun came like gold through the trees, and over the fields, and I felt like I was in heaven."

But freedom wasn't heaven. The very next year Congress passed the Fugitive Slave Law of 1850, making it a crime for anyone to help a runaway slave and stating that runaway slaves, if found, could be returned to their masters in the South. Harriet couldn't sit back and enjoy freedom for herself. She had to go back and get her family.

In December of 1850, Harriet went back the way she had come and safely brought her sister Mary and Mary's husband and two children to freedom. The following spring, Harriet went back and led her brother and two other men to safety. That fall she went back a third time, disguised as a man, to get her husband—only to discover that John Tubman had taken another wife! Deeply hurt, she nonetheless gathered together a small group of slaves and led them north.

Now Harriet's motives changed. Before she had come back only to lead her family to freedom; now she took anyone who wanted to flee. She became a legend, both feared and admired. Who was this mysterious person the slaves called "Moses," who spirited away the slaves? Many thought she was a man.

During her lifetime Harriet Tubman led at least three hundred men, women, and children to safety over the Underground Railroad, including her aging parents, Ben and Old 'Rit. The trips got longer and more dangerous because of the numerous slave catchers out looking for runaways. Now she had to lead her small bands all the way to Canada. "But I never lost a passenger," she said proudly. By 1860, the reward for her capture had reached a staggering $60,000.

In November 1860, Abraham Lincoln was elected president of the United States. Within a year, eleven southern states had seceded and formed a new union: the Confederate States of America. Soon Harriet, who had settled in Auburn, New York, had a new role as scout, spy, and even "nurse" (making use of her woodlore knowledge of healing herbs) for the Union Army. But even though Harriet Tubman was highly respected and given many privileges during the war, she never received any of the back pay due her for her services to the Union Army.

The Civil War ended on April 9, 1865. Abraham Lincoln was assassinated six nights later. In December 1865, the Thirteenth Amendment was ratified. At last a dream had come true: slavery was dead.

Two years after the war ended, Harriet learned that her former husband, John Tubman, had been murdered. Even though she was only forty-seven years old, she felt old and lonely for the family life she never had. But two years later she married a black war veteran named Nelson Davis, who was twenty years younger than Harriet. Davis had tuberculosis and was virtually an invalid; he died at the age of forty-four after nineteen years of marriage.

During this time, Mrs. Sarah Hopkins Bradford, an Auburn schoolteacher, wrote and published two books about Harriet Tubman: *Scenes in the Life of Harriet Tubman* (1868) and *Harriet, the Moses of Her People* (1886). Mrs. Bradford donated the royalties from the books to Harriet, who used the money to establish a home for the sick, poor, and homeless. Harriet also earned money by raising and selling vegetables house to house in Auburn. Sometimes she didn't get much selling done, because each customer wanted to give her a cup of buttered tea and hear stories of her adventures on the Underground Railroad.

In 1903, Harriet donated her home and twenty-five acres of land to the African Methodist Episcopal (AME) Church of Auburn, though she continued to live there herself. Against her wishes, the AME Church began to charge a fee to the Home's residents.

On March 10, 1913, Harriet Tubman died at the age of ninety-three. The citizens of Auburn, New York, erected a bronze tablet outside the courthouse, which reads:

IN MEMORY OF HARRIET TUBMAN.

BORN A SLAVE IN MARYLAND ABOUT 1821.

DIED IN AUBURN, N.Y., MARCH 10TH, 1913.

CALLED THE MOSES OF HER PEOPLE,

DURING THE CIVIL WAR. WITH RARE

COURAGE SHE LED OVER THREE HUNDRED

NEGROES UP FROM SLAVERY TO FREEDOM,

AND RENDERED INVALUABLE SERVICE

AS NURSE AND SPY.

WITH IMPLICIT TRUST IN GOD

SHE BRAVED EVERY DANGER AND

OVERCAME EVERY OBSTACLE. WITHAL

SHE POSSESSED EXTRAORDINARY

FORESIGHT AND JUDGMENT SO THAT

SHE TRUTHFULLY SAID

"ON MY UNDERGROUND RAILROAD

I NEBBER RUN MY TRAIN OFF DE TRACK

AN' I NEBBER LOS' A PASSENGER."

THIS TABLET IS ERECTED

BY THE CITIZENS OF AUBURN.

For Further Reading

Bains, Rae. *Harriet Tubman: The Road to Freedom*. Mahwah, N.J.: Troll Associates, 1982.

Burns, Bree. *Harriet Tubman*. [New York]: Chelsea Juniors, 1992. Part of the Junior World Biographies. Includes bibliographical references and index.

Elish, Dan. *Harriet Tubman and the Underground Railroad*. Brookfield, Conn.: Millbrook Press, 1993. Gateway Civil Rights series. Includes bibliographical references and index.

Ferris, Jeri. *Go Free or Die: A Story about Harriet Tubman*. Minneapolis: Carolrhoda House, 1988. A Carolrhoda Creative Minds book.

Humphreville, Frances T. *Harriet Tubman: Flame of Freedom*. Boston, Houghton Mifflin, 1967. Piper Books series.

McGovern, Ann. *"Wanted Dead or Alive": The True Story of Harriet Tubman*. New York: Scholastic Book Services, 1965. (Also published under the title: *Runaway Slave, the Story of Harriet Tubman*. New York: Four Winds Press, 1965.)

McMullan, Kate. *The Story of Harriet Tubman: Conductor of the Underground Railroad*. New York: Dell Publishing, 1991. A Dell Yearling biography.